Out of This Nettle

Jean Ducey

Baker Book House
Grand Rapids, Michigan 49506

ISBN: 0–8010–2927–9

Printed in the United States of America

For
Michelle, Brie, Mark, and Seth
and in memory of their ancestors,
Cornelius and Susannah Stephens Sparks,
who so despised slavery

Contents

Preface

Jane Van Vliet published the abolition paper, The *Star of Freedom,* in Niles, Michigan, for a period of four months in 1845. Sam Gunn was active in slave stealing then. Nearly all of the characters were living and working in the precisely named occupations. The Shakers of Berrien Springs, however, have been moved up thirteen years in time. The newspaper quotations are from the papers of the day and the council notes used are the actual notes.

Out of this nettle, danger, we pluck this flower, safety.

King Henry IV, Part I [2.3.11]

1

February, 1845—
A Snowball Changes
Neil's Life

No one had ever seen such an odd snowstorm, not even Miss Meachum. She gave the children permission to leave their seats and watch from the small window. No one looked at the snow, however, until first searching for Fats, for this was the time of day when he usually made his appearance. Even the girls watched for him. Though he did no more than trip them, or fill their stocking caps with snow, it was frightening to hear the maniacal yell that always accompanied his attacks.

Neil also watched for Fats as he, peering over the heads of the smaller students, took his turn at the window. He had fallen victim to Fats's tormenting on his first day at school after coming to stay with Aunt Annie and Uncle Bert. He had no wish to repeat the experience.

"Oh, we've a pretty boy here now, haven't we?" Fats had yelled, twisting Neil's arm until he felt it would leave the shoulder socket. Fighting to get away, he caught a glimpse of the round face in which the eyes were shifty and sly. Only later did he see the huge ring of fat around Fats's middle—so great a shelf that his arms could rest upon it. There was no way to fight

9

such fat, especially when those arms were so much longer, the shoulders so much wider and higher than Neil's own.

Though Neil was twelve and rarely cried, he had cried a little that day as, hurting with each step, he forced himself up the hill. His eye was swelling shut and he felt he would never be able to lift his arm again. He tried to count his teeth with his tongue. No one had ever called him "pretty boy" and that hurt, too. Dark hair and freckles certainly couldn't make one pretty, but Neil felt being slight might mean pretty to anyone shaped like Fats.

At the moment, however, Fats was nowhere visible. Neil shook his head, scattering his unhappy memories. He watched the flakes floating lazily down, enormous flakes. He judged most to be three inches across. Touching one another, they clung, forming huge circles and melting instantly on meeting the damp ground.

Miss Meachum came to look over Neil's shoulder. She was alarmed at the sudden gray of the sky. Myriads of the large flakes were now piling so quickly that they could no longer melt.

"Hurry, children. Leave your copybooks. Get your coats and go straight home. Oh, Cornelius, you should have worn boots!"

Neil wasn't thinking about boots; he knew that a wet snow was a packing snow and he hurried out to scoop up a snowball, stopping first to intercept from the quiet deluge one delicate flake, so like Queen Anne's lace. He wondered if this same snow could be falling six miles away, at home? And if his father had recovered from the scarlet fever? If so, was he hurrying to get the cows in? Was Shep helping, nipping at their heels? Neil smiled when he thought of such a large snowflake settling on Shep's nose and was suddenly stabbed with homesickness.

"Aunt Annie will be watching for me," he thought, "but maybe Clay and I can throw some snowballs before I start home."

Neil tramped down Sycamore Street hill, stopping only to watch men brake a wagon to keep it from sliding into the oxen. Packing a snowball, he made his way through the deepening snow toward Nigger Bill's barbershop. Crossing Front Street, brushing the snow from his eyes, he could just make out a burly figure with a smaller boy—Fats Gunn with his afternoon victim!

"It's Clay! He's snagged onto Clay!" Neil's stomach felt sick as he watched his friend bend toward the ground under Fats's tightening grip. Neil heard Fats: "You stay on your own side of the street, nigger, or I'll send you back where you belong!"

Neil knew that he and Clay together—the both of them—couldn't beat Fats, but that he must, somehow, help Clay. With a final hard pack he sent the icy snowball straight for the back of Fats's head. Splat! It hit with such force that Fats's arms were flung wide; he slipped and went down on his back with a yell.

In that moment while Fats struggled to his feet, Clay ran toward the river and Neil tore for the alley. Rounding the corner, he skidded against steps. With hope in his heart, he bounded up the steps and lifted the door latch. The door opened and he slipped inside, sliding the bar home. Leaning against it, catching his breath,

11

Neil prayed the heavy snow was covering his foot-prints.

The hope was vain. Soon a pounding came. Neil held his breath, wondering whose business he had stepped into. At the far end of the long storeroom a door opened. Framed in the light was a young woman in a dark dress with a white collar and long, stiff cuffs.

"Did you knock? You wanted to buy a paper?" Her voice was pleasantly low.

Afraid that Fats might knock again, Neil moved quickly toward her. "Yes, ma'am, but I don't have any money."

She laughed, ushering him into a room pungent with the scent of paper and ink. "Perhaps we can put you to work for a copy. Mr. Rogers, our prayers for a delivery boy may have been answered."

Looking up from the long table where he was tying papers into rolls, Mr. Rogers peered at Neil from beneath his eyeshade. Then he smiled and Neil thought him a handsome man with his silver hair, though his black, bushy eyebrows were a surprise.

"Think you can manage in this snow, son?"

"Yes, sir."

"Fine. This is our first edition and we're anxious that these three deliveries be made today. This is for Mr. LaPierre at the jewelry store. This second roll is for Mr. Lord at the Presbyterian church, and the third goes to Dr. Finley across from the school. Can you find them?"

"Yes, sir, I know where they are." Indeed Neil knew;

there was no alley or lane or swamp in the village that he and Clay had not explored.

"And where do you live?" the young woman asked.

"I'm staying with my aunt and uncle beyond Fifth Street."

"Well, you'd best get started then. What is your name?"

"Cornelius Sparks."

"Here is a paper for you, Cornelius. Do you think you will be able to help us tomorrow?"

"I'll ask my aunt and uncle, ma'am."

"Do you think they might let you work after school and on Saturday, too? You do go to school?"

Smiling and nodding a hurried yes to each question, Neil picked up the rolls of papers, opened the front door, and stepped out on the stoop. An ominous figure waited at the corner.

"Here we go," Neil thought and kept on his way.

"It was you hit me with that snowball, and I'm goin' to get you for it," Fats yelled.

Neil yelled right back, "You gone crazy? I'm working. You let me alone or I'll get the marshal!"

Fats was momentarily taken aback. Then he walked along, taunting, "The marshal don't care what I do! You workin' for that nigger lover? You'd never catch me workin' for no woman! Anytime I'd ever. . . ."

Neil stepped as rapidly as he could and was glad to dodge into the jewelry shop. Mr. LaPierre looked up from his desk at the window. "If that's young Gunn out there, I'd advise you stay clear of him."

13

Neil agreed fervently as he brushed the snow off the papers. "Could I go out your back door, sir?"

"Come through here, young man. It is good of you to make a delivery in such a storm. We've waited a long time for this paper." The jeweler removed the little glasses pinched tight to his nose and smiled. "What a feast my eyes will have tonight!"

As Neil cut up the alley and over to Church Street, he was puzzled. "What kind of paper is it? What is Mr. LaPierre going to feast on?"

Knocking at the parsonage door of the Reverend Charles Lord, Neil mused, "I never thought about his name before; that's a good one for a minister." Mr. Lord's housekeeper took the papers and Neil went, as fast as the snow allowed, over to Sycamore Street hill. Halfway down the hill, across from the school, he delivered the last roll. Neil politely refused Mrs. Finley's offer of a cup of hot cider, for he was anxious to get home.

Ploughing his way back up the hill, Neil rehearsed his explanation. He would stress that he had been working, that he had earned this paper, since work was next to godliness with Aunt Annie.

Yet, when Neil suddenly appeared out of the snowy dark, Aunt Annie was so relieved that she did little except fuss over his wet clothing. She made him stand on the rug while she and Uncle Bert took proper care of each garment.

"Maybe at home you can throw your clothes any which way, but not in this house."

Neil did not want to offend Aunt Annie now that things seemed to be going smoothly. When he had first

14

come to stay he could do nothing right. He slammed doors, forgot to clean his boots on the scraper, forgot to wash his hands, put too much food in his mouth, and sulked, Aunt Annie said, when he was reminded. Now that the worst of his homesickness was over things seemed to have settled somewhat.

If he had been late at home his mother likely wouldn't even have missed him, but Aunt Annie was different. How, Neil pondered, could two people such as Aunt Annie and his mother, who must be the world's worst housekeeper, ever wind up as sisters?

Neil got his shoes off and Aunt Annie shook her head. "Land sakes alive, but these will be a time drying, and stiff as a board they'll be. It will take all three of us to get them back on, like as not." She stuffed them with rags before placing them behind the stove.

"Oats would do better than those rags," Uncle Bert said. "I'll bring some in tomorrow morning."

As they ate, Neil related each exciting detail of the afternoon.

"I'm glad your aim was good, Neil," Aunt Annie said. "I don't know why those folks raise that boy as they do. Just because he's an only child is no reason to spoil him so. Pity they never sent him to school."

"Is Mr. Gunn fat, too?"

"No, but Mrs. Gunn has certainly let herself go, she's as round as a house."

Uncle Bert said, "I'm glad you were able to help Bill Rogers, Neil. He's a fine man."

"How old is Mr. Rogers, Uncle Bert? His hair is white, but his eyebrows are black and he's not fat at all."

"Bill's older than I am by about fifteen years—he's close to fifty-five. If you want to help them till this snow clears that's fine, Neil, so long as you understand it may be a thorny job. A lot of feeling around against anyone who wants to help the slaves."

Neil was decisive. "I want to help."

Then Uncle Bert spread the first weekly edition of the *Star of Freedom* on the table and read parts aloud, saving some for the coming nights.

The snow was still drifting down as Neil undressed for bed. He knew there would be no school the next day, but he hoped he could find some thick socks to go inside his boots until his shoes dried, for he'd promised to help Miss Van Vliet. He knew her name now since Uncle Bert had read it:

The *Star of Freedom* will be published every Wednesday morning in Niles, Berrien County, Michigan, for the Michigan State Anti-Slavery Society. Jane Van Vliet, Printer. Terms, $2.00 per annum, in advance. $2.50 in six months. $3.00 if payment be delayed to the close of the year. A strict adherence to the above terms will be observed in every case. Advertisements thankfully received and inserted at the usual prices in this vicinity. Any friend of humanity desiring to aid the cause of Liberty is authorized to act as Agent.

Neil had never heard much about slavery. Since listening to Uncle Bert reading the paper, his head was whirling with thoughts about it. He remembered his father saying he'd never eat with a nigger—but when Mr. Johnson's man, Julius Caesar, came to help with the threshing his mother asked him to sit at table with the rest of the men. His father had been forced to sit down without saying anything.

As Neil climbed into bed he grinned, thinking about the snowball that freed Clay and sent Fats reeling. "Hey," he suddenly remembered, "it landed pretty close to the spot where Clay saved my life—just about a year ago, too! Maybe I helped repay him."

Snuggling down under the warm covers, Neil still shivered as he thought of the cold that long-ago afternoon. "Must have been the last Sunday in March because that's when little Ada was born and Millie and I were staying here."

He recalled his relief when his sister decided to stay with Aunt Annie. "Now I won't have her trailing along after me," he thought, and ran all the way to the river so as not to be late to watch the Baptists at their baptizing.

Aunt Annie had explained, "The Baptists consider we are only partial Christians because we are sprinkled, not immersed."

Uncle Bert told Neil why the Baptists chose this spot in the river for their baptizing. "It's the only low place—it was where the Indians waded across. We called it the 'Crossing,' but the Indians called it 'Pawating.' It's a narrow passage at best, a poor way to cross, a dangerous way, and when the river was in flood, it was impossible to cross."

"No bridge then, Uncle Bert?"

"No. Before the bridge we had a ferry, or used canoes."

"Did you help build the bridge, Uncle Bert?"

"No, I subscribed money. Everybody did."

17

Neil headed for the big sycamore tree overhanging the St. Joseph River; he judged it would be directly opposite the baptistery. People were already clustered on the bridge when he climbed up into the tree, and soon four older boys decided to join him, pushing Neil out to the end of the limb.

The pastor, aided by one of his deacons, walked down into the water, waist deep. He turned, facing the parishioners gathered on the bank, and opened his Bible. Neil thought he would be unable to hear, but the pastor's deep voice rolled out across the water:

Then cometh Jesus from Galilee to Jordan unto John, to be baptized of him. But John forbad him, saying, I have need to be baptized of thee, and comest thou to me? And Jesus answering said unto him, Suffer it to be so now; for thus it becometh us to fulfil all righteousness. Then he suffered him. And Jesus, when he was baptized, went up straightway out of the water; and lo, the heavens were opened unto him, and he saw the Spirit of God descending like a dove, and lighting upon Him: And lo a voice from heaven, saying, This is my beloved Son, in whom I am well pleased.

Another deacon led a man into the water, and the pastor began, "Having accepted the Lord Jesus Christ as your Redeemer, I baptize you, my brother, in the name of the Father, and of the Son, and of the Holy Ghost."

As the believer was gently lowered into the water, those on the bank sang,

Baptize the nations; far and nigh
The triumphs of the cross record;
The name of Jesus glorify
Till every kindred call him Lord.

The last to be baptized was a plump girl who suddenly panicked and fought against being put under water. She struggled and plunged about and the pastor had a difficult time until the deacon held her arms. Together they managed to get her underneath the water, except for her nose.

This unusual climax to the ceremony caused great snickering and jostling among the boys on the limb. Their laughter covered the protesting limb's sharp, splintering crack as the big branch with its load of lively spectators suddenly pitched into the river.

Later Clay told Neil of the confused scene: "There was lots of legs and arms and splashing and yelling. All of 'em bobbed up but you. Men jumped in from this end of the bridge, but I don't think anyone but me knew how many were on the limb. I knew you were still down and I must have jumped in the right spot 'cause I touched your leg right soon. When I pulled you up I yelled and treaded water till men came back from the other bank to help."

Once they had him ashore, the men put Neil over the knees of the Reverend Day, who pumped the water out of his lungs with a vigor usually reserved for meting out discipline. Then they lifted him to his feet and Mr. Day looked into his eyes and examined his head.

"You've a nasty bump, son. Fortunate for you that

your friend here pulled you up when he did. Men, walk these two boys up to my wagon."

Mrs. Day hurried along, settling herself between the boys, putting one lap robe about their legs, holding another about their shoulders. "Hurry, Mr. Day, or they'll catch their deaths."

Urging his horse across the bridge and through the Triangle, Mr. Day jested, "If I had been quicker, I could have had a few more fresh-made Christians, couldn't I?"

Clay and Neil sealed their friendship with shy glances and grins. Neil knew he would never forget Clay's eyes so long as he lived. It was his first acquaintance with a young Negro. "I'm owing to him," Neil thought.

As Mr. Day stopped beside the barbershop and helped Clay down, hurrying him inside, Neil lifted his hand in farewell. Then they turned up Sycamore Street hill and out Fifth Street.

"Make haste, Mr. Day."

Mr. Day did as his wife instructed and was soon telling Aunt Annie all that had happened, urging her to give Neil something hot to drink lest he catch cold.

"Keep him active, ma'am, don't put him to bed."

Directly Aunt Annie had stripped Neil of his muddy, still-dripping clothing. She toweled his hair dry. Then, after he was in a dry suit of underwear and wrapped in Uncle Bert's robe, she bade him tell the whole story as she went to work, though it was the Sabbath, making mince pies and nut bread. That very evening, Uncle Bert delivered one of each, still warm, to Mrs. Day and Clay's father, with his thanks.

"Mr. and Mrs. Day," Uncle Bert told Aunt Annie

later, "are certainly fine people. This village is lucky to have them here."

"I allow some Baptists are more decent as others," Aunt Annie said.

In a few days Neil went to the barbershop to pick up the pie tin and Clay walked him partway home, along the river. They had been fast friends since and, through the year, whenever Neil came to the village with his father, he stopped to play with Clay.

Now, in bed, in the quiet of the night, Neil tried to relive that wrenching experience, to push his memory beyond the point were his head hit the rock. He could not—always the rock blacked out every sensation after the shock of falling in backward and helpless, with his nose and mouth filling with cold water, and the panic of the sudden weight of his clothing pulling him down.

Neil turned on his side and pulled the cover over his ear. As sleep came he thought, "I'll be sure to see Clay tomorrow . . . tell him about the snowball . . . about Miss Van Vliet. . . ."

2

A Heady Beginning

The next morning Neil found three thick pairs of woolen socks warming beside his own long stockings on the chair next to the sitting-room stove. His steps were so comfortably cushioned that he hoped his shoes took a long time drying.

Not for the first time he reflected that life with Aunt Annie was easy compared with life at home on the farm. Neil could never remember seeing Aunt Annie with her hands empty, nor his mother for that matter. But their hands held different things. Aunt Annie generally held a dishcloth, a hoe, or a broom, while his mother quite often used a fishing pole, or a pen to write a poem. His mother was slender and beautiful and moved like quicksilver—necessary, for she never began any task until much too late. He was sure Aunt Annie would make two of his mother and her round face couldn't rightly be called pretty, but she went her calm, unhurried way, always working well ahead of the clock.

Now Aunt Annie called to him, as she sliced potatoes, "The snow was still coming down hard, Neil, at four this morning."

In the warm kitchen, fragrant with frying ham, Neil

took his jacket from the hook. "I'll get a path shoveled to the barn right away, Aunt Annie."

After the chores and the shoveling Uncle Bert and Neil came in, stamping the snow away. Uncle Bert brushed the flakes from his mustache and took from his pocket a small bag of oats, which Aunt Annie promptly transferred to Neil's wet shoes. They sat down to a breakfast of ham and eggs, potatoes fried in the ham fat, applesauce, and mince pie left from supper.

Then Uncle Bert hitched Bessie to the cutter and they were away, gliding through a white and silent world where the only evidence of life lay in the smoke curling up from the chimneys, each with its knotting of sparrows.

Neil felt he knew Uncle Bert much better this morning. Until their talk last night about his working for Miss Van Vliet, he assumed Uncle Bert had always lived in Niles.

"No," Uncle Bert had explained, "I was eight years old when we moved from North Carolina to Indiana and it wasn't until I was eighteen that I came to work here, clearing land at ten dollars an acre. After two months at that, I went to work keelboating on the river so as to make more money. That was when I met your Aunt Annie."

"You met her on the river?"

"No, Neil," Aunt Annie said, "a friend of your mother's had a new music book—songs that weren't hymns—so she invited some of us over to sing. Your Uncle Bert was there, too."

Uncle Bert grinned, "Your Aunt Annie had the prettiest voice I ever heard and she could sing harmony.

24

But I soon found out she was not about to marry a riverman, so I quit keelboating and went to laying the road to St. Joe."

"We saved and bought eighty acres here and your Uncle Bert cut the logs to build this house."

"Whatever you do for Miss Van Vliet, Neil, you'll be starting out easier than I did. My first day in Niles I hired out to drive cattle and I worked from four o'clock in the morning without a bite to eat until supper at night."

"Why didn't you stop to eat?"

"Because you have to keep the cattle moving. I fast learned to carry apples in my pockets!"

Now, at Front Street, they met other men in sleighs and cutters calling out the latest news of the storm. Miss Van Vliet saw them pull up outside and came to the door, smiling. She had liked the bright look of this boy that moment yesterday when he said he would like a paper but had no money for a copy, and she trusted her first judgment. Uncle Bert came into the office and was introduced.

"I'm pleased to meet you, Mr. Jarvis, and I am so glad to see Cornelius again."

Mr. Rogers came out of the pressroom. "I thought I recognized that voice! How are you, Bert?"

"Fine, Bill. Glad to see you back here."

Miss Van Vliet explained, "Mr. Jarvis is uncle to Cornelius."

Mr. Rogers was surprised. "Well, that certainly knocks the whole thing into pie! I thought we'd found a good helper last night—now I'm sure of it."

Uncle Bert explained, "Neil is quarantined out of

home—scarlet fever. He'd been helping a neighbor when the doctor came by and told him not to go home. So they brought him to stay with us."

"Mr. Jarvis, could Cornelius help us after school and Saturdays, too?"

"Yes, ma'am, that's all right, but I've warned him it could be a troublesome job."

"I'm glad you did, though we don't know yet how much trouble we may have."

After Uncle Bert left, Miss Van Vliet asked, "Would twelve cents a week in salary be satisfactory to start, Cornelius?"

"Yes, ma'am." Neil thought quickly, "That will be forty-eight cents a month!"

"Fine. The most important thing this morning is to get as many papers delivered as possible. With this snow it will be hard going. But first, could you shovel the steps and paths? And fill the woodboxes?"

As Neil finished the shoveling and climbed the steps, a snowball whizzed by, smashing against the door, missing his head. Without looking toward the street, he pressed the latch and stepped inside.

"Just like yesterday," he thought, and he knew Fats Gunn hadn't forgotten yesterday, either.

Miss Van Vliet came out to the back room. "The papers are ready to go to the post office, Cornelius. I'll get the bag for you."

Prudently, Neil folded a paper into a small, thick square and placed it inside his stocking cap. He was happy that he did not encounter Fats on the short walk.

26

Postmaster Chester's friendly greeting cooled when he peered into the bag. "You one of these slavocrats?"

Neil was embarrassed at this loud question before the men lounging at the post office. He was uncomfortably aware of a man waiting quietly behind him.

Mr. Chester advised, "Look, boy, you've asked for trouble with that outfit. Your Miss Van Vliet would be a lot smarter if she'd get back to her knitting where she belongs. But the law says I've got to mail the dirty rag." He emptied the bag onto the counter and inspected the addresses.

"And I want these papers picked up every week without fail. With all the printers mailing free to each other, the papers get stacked up around here. And here's a list of names of folks who need to pick up their letters; you can give it to Miss Van Vliet to print."

Packing the incoming papers into the bag, Neil thanked the postmaster and was glad to escape. He was thinking of Uncle Bert's prediction of trouble when the man who had been behind him at the post office window caught up and fell in step.

"If you're working for Miss Van Vliet you'll be neighbor to me. That's my shoe shop next door. Ancel Hawkins."

Neil noticed that Ancel's neat, dapper mustache turned up on the ends, making a smile of its own. "Glad to know you, sir. My name's Cornelius Sparks."

"When you deliver my paper, Cornelius, I'd rather you left it at the shop and not at my house."

"Where do you live, sir?"

Ancel pointed up to the big house at the top of Church Street hill.

"At least," Neil thought as Ancel stepped into his shop, "Mr. Hawkins cancels our Mr. Chester's orneriness." Returning to the office, Neil explained the list from Mr. Chester and exchanged sacks of papers with Miss Van Vliet.

"These, Cornelius, go to the subscribers on Third Street and down Bond Street. Each one is addressed. When you get back, I want you take time to eat before you deliver more."

Neil passed the steam mill and headed up Church Street hill. When he reached Ancel Hawkins's big house, he turned and looked down at the river flowing along like a black ribbon between high snowbanks. From the hilltop the village looked like a toy and he felt as though he were a giant. His musing was interrupted by the pealing notes of the tin horn blown by the stage driver, Three-fingered Jack, approaching Niles from Berrien Springs. The notes woke the village. As the echoes died away in the forests, doors opened; people appeared to witness the coming in of the stage and to hear the news of the outer world. The giant on the hill turned his attention to delivering papers.

As Neil finished his route he heard the stage behind him with a fresh hitch of horses, heading down Bond Street hill on the way to Bertrand. A horse and cutter were partway up the hill and the man in the cutter yelled, "I'm nearly at the top of the hill, why don't you back and allow me passage?"

Jack didn't feel that way about it. He patted his padlocked leather mailbag and said, "Uncle Sam don't want this little satchel detained, mister!"

Shrugging his shoulders, the single driver sidestepped

his horse over to the edge of the hill. Neil grinned and waited to catch a ride. Once he saw a figure behind the trees and thought of Fats. When he looked back, however, he saw no one.

At the bottom of Main Street hill he hopped out with thanks and made his way to the office. Mr. Rogers asked, "Cornelius, before you take off your jacket, would you cross the street and show this notice to Judge Brown? I can't read his writing! It looks like a haystack that's been struck by a cyclone."

Chuckling, Neil took the sheet and climbed the stairs to the judge's office over the bookstore. Judge Brown finally found his glasses on the top of his head and peered through them, puzzling over the notice. Then he asked, "What crazy fool wrote this?"

Neil returned with the corrected paper, laughing as he reported the judge's comment. Mr. Rogers shook his head. "Poor Jim, a victim of too much corn juice. Be a good thing if they raised the price to four cents a glass."

While Miss Van Vliet tended the office, Neil and Mr. Rogers ate. Neil unwound the huge cinnamon roll Aunt Annie had packed and found Mr. Rogers watching in fascination. Neil broke off a large piece. "Would you like some, sir? Aunt Annie always packs way too much for one person."

"I haven't tasted anything like this for years," Mr. Rogers said. "I wish Lutie could cook like Annie Jarvis."

"Lutie, sir?"

"Lutie Bibbins, my landlady." Mr. Rogers shook his head in sorrow. "She's a terrible cook."

"May I disturb you a minute?" Miss Van Vliet asked. "I want to show you two clippings. This is from the *New York Sun.* Evidently they don't approve of me."

Lady Editor

Miss Jane Van Vliet edits the *Star of Freedom,* a Liberty Paper in Niles, Michigan. A contemporary quietly asks, "Who does her knitting and mending?"

Mr. Rogers read it to Neil, shaking his head.

"And this one is from the *Emancipator,* in reply to the *Sun,* and they are defending me!"

Again Mr. Rogers read aloud:

Bonaparte quietly asked a similar question of Madame de Stael; but nobody admires his wisdom for it. Somebody put a similar interrogatory once to Hannah More, but the people of England have answered the question.

Neil was puzzled. "Who are they?"

"They were famous writers, Neil."

Neil doubted that they were any better than Miss Van Vliet. He knew they couldn't have been as pretty as she was, with her dark hair parted in the middle and drawn back to a figure eight in back. "Everything about her is neat, nothing crooked. If people expect her to be bossy because she's in business, they're going to be surprised."

Mr. Rogers stood up and stretched and Neil went to pack his bag with papers to deliver out to the Yankee Street branch-off. Again, on the way, he thought he saw a figure in the trees and determined to watch more carefully on the return trip. He saw no one, however, and concluded that he must have been imagining. He didn't remove the paper from his hat, though.

"Cornelius," Miss Van Vliet asked the moment he came in, "do you think school will be in session tomorrow?"

"No, ma'am. Not till this snow begins to melt."

"That will help us; the boy we were planning on has the mumps and won't be able to work for some time. And you will be deserving of more pay if you can work full time."

Secretly pleased, Neil gave a businesslike nod. The bell on the door jingled then as Ancel Hawkins came to place an advertisement for his shoe shop. Once the ad was read and corrected, Neil noticed that Ancel seemed in no hurry to leave.

Miss Van Vliet was brisk, however. "Thank you very much, Mr. Hawkins. That is a generous ad and you may be sure it will appear in next week's edition. It will continue until we hear differently. If you will excuse me, I'll give this to Mr. Rogers."

When Ancel left, Miss Van Vliet said, "Mr. Rogers, Mr. Hawkins paid in cash, not in potatoes or in wood, and he's paid for an entire year."

Mr. Rogers was puzzled. "I wonder what made him change his mind? He was definite about not needing an ad when I asked him."

For a long moment they looked at one another and Neil remembered that Uncle Bert had told him that Ancel's big house on the hill was the only one in the village with running water. Neil had gone to see the spring under the foot of the bridge and the hydraulic ram that rattled there continually, sending the water in pipes up the hill and into the house.

Uncle Bert also said that Ancel had come to the village with just a kit of cobbler's tools eleven years ago and now his trade had grown so much that he employed twelve cobblers and that he'd gotten all the village shoemakers to build their own tannery.

"He is a go-getter; he's built thirty houses in this village."

"And," Aunt Annie commented shrewdly, "he'll never get married until he finds a gal as rich as he is."

During the rest of the afternoon Neil swept the rooms, filled the paste pots, and laid out candles. Mr. Rogers showed him how type was set, holding the stick in his left hand and using his thumb to keep the growing line in place. He promised to let Neil set type soon. Without being told, Neil could see the importance of spelling and sentence construction.

"How did you learn to set type, Mr. Rogers?"

"I began just the way you are, Neil, back in New York, at about your age, sweeping and running errands. For four years I was taught the trade and I was expected to value my instruction more than my wages."

Suddenly Neil had an idea, a great idea; he thought that suppertime would be the best time to mention it.

As soon as Uncle Bert asked the blessing, Neil told Aunt Annie how much Mr. Rogers had enjoyed her cinnamon roll, and what the *New York Sun* had said about Miss Van Vliet.

Aunt Annie was pleased about Mr. Roger's compliment, but her lips came together in disapproval over the *Sun's* comment.

"If Miss Van Vliet has neither chick nor child to look after, I see no reason why she shouldn't print a paper. Those men editors don't want to admit a woman can do it, besides which, the real reason they're upset is that she's brave enough to talk about slavery when they aren't. That's the whole truth—they'd rather line their pocketbooks and sweep slavery under the rug."

"I have a hard time thinking of her as Miss Van Vliet," Uncle Bert said. "She's so young. She can't be more than eighteen."

"Mr. Rogers calls her Jane," Neil said.

"Well, he knew her as a child. Of course, you'll call her ma'am or Miss Van Vliet," Aunt Annie reminded him.

"Aunt Annie, how long does it take to get over the mumps?"

"Depends. Quite a time, usually. Don't tell me you're getting mumps?"

"No, but the boy who was going to help Miss Van Vliet has them. They need me real bad, Aunt Annie. I wish I could keep working for them instead of going back to school. I'd learn just as much. I think I'd learn more," Neil said passionately.

"Well, now," Uncle Bert said, "I don't know what your father would say to that."

"He wouldn't care as long as I'd be home in time to help with planting."

"When you go home depends on when the quarantine is lifted," Aunt Annie said. "If your sisters get the fever, and they likely will, that might be quite a spell."

"What do you do first when you get to school, Neil?" Uncle Bert asked.

"About nine we read from the Testament. Then we have arithmetic and reading and spelling. Afternoons we have the same, only we start with spelling and then reading and arithmetic."

"What do you study on Saturdays?"

"We only go every other Saturday, and we have the same over again. I'll be learning arithmetic when I collect for the paper. Mr. Rogers is going to show me how to set type, and I learn spelling just reading papers. Today I learned about Madame de Stael and Hannah More. And I learn about geography—we never have that in school. Mr. Rogers said he was just my age when he started in printing. And Miss Van Vliet said I should get more pay if I worked full time, so I could pay room and board. Please, Uncle Bert!"

"No need to pay, Neil," Uncle Bert said, "you save your money."

Aunt Annie thought it out. "The boy is earning money. He may be learning important things, and we should read the Testament at night, anyway. I think you should tell Miss Meachum he won't be back, for now, Bert?"

Uncle Bert nodded. "Lucky I didn't take any more wood over to school."

"I'll write your mother, Neil, and tell her what we've done. If your folks don't like it, we'll put you back in school. No telling when they'll get to Berrien to pick up the letter, though. Well, that's decided. You read to us from the paper, Bert, while Neil and I do up these dishes."

Neil slowly let out his breath. He doubted that he would ever again do dishes so willingly, in such happiness.

Uncle Bert read a letter written by Jonathan Walker from the Pensacola jail. "Evidently he's being held for helping slaves to escape. Here is what he says: 'Out of 256 days solitary confinement in this place, I have been 173 days in heavy irons.'"

Neil and Aunt Annie looked at one another in shock. "Go on, Bert."

"Here's a happier note—a quotation from Shakespeare:

> There's a divinity that shapes our ends,
> Rough-hew them how we will."

"Hamlet," Aunt Annie said, hanging up the dishcloth. "That's one of my favorites."

She brought her mending to the table and Uncle Bert changed over to Mr. Cook's paper, the *Niles Republican:*

Star of Freedom is the title of a new paper which has made its appearance on our table published in this village and edited by Miss Jane Van Vliet. Its object is to advance the cause of political abolitionism. We wish the lady success in her undertaking, so far as fat jobs and a good living is concerned. But political

35

abolitionism we still look upon as calculated to promote anything but good results and we believe if the agitation of the question of slavery would cease at the North the country would be rid of the evil much earlier.

"What," Neil asked, "does he mean? What's political abolitionism?"

"Forget that word *political,*" Aunt Annie advised. "Politics should have nothing to do with slavery, because God doesn't. No place in the Bible will you find that it's right to enslave another human being. That's all abolitionism means—abolish slavery."

Aunt Annie put away her mending. "Now you write a letter to your folks, Neil, before you go to bed, and I'll put it in with mine."

Neil wrote,

Dear Mama and Papa:

I miss you and Shep too. I hope Papa is over the fever and that no one else has it. I have a fine job and am earning money which I will save most of. I hope that is all right. I am going to learn how to set type. I hang up my clothes here all the time.

Your son, Neil

He undressed behind the stove, holding the warm flannel nightgown close around him for the dash through the cold to his room. Once in bed, his toes sought the warmth of the hot brick Aunt Annie had wrapped in layers and layers of thick wool.

He lay content, knowing that he would be helping

Miss Van Vliet and Mr. Rogers all day, every day. He hoped morning would come soon so that he could tell them they needn't worry anymore about help.

Two random thoughts surfaced. Aunt Annie had said it was likely his sisters would get the scarlet fever. He hoped not, especially not little Ada. And he remembered the long look that had passed between Miss Van Vliet and Mr. Rogers when she announced that Ancel Hawkins had paid, a year in advance, for his ad. "Why weren't they pleased at cash in hand?"

3

A Printer's Devil

The snowrollers had not yet been out to Fifth Street, so Uncle Bert hitched Bessie to the cutter and took Neil to work the next morning. The moment Neil was inside the door he called, "Miss Van Vliet, I'm going to help all the time! I'm not going back to school and Aunt Annie and Uncle Bert say it's all right."

Turning from her desk, Miss Van Vliet clapped her hands, "Oh, Neil, that's wonderful!"

There was no need to tell Mr. Rogers. Smiling, he said that he'd heard every word. Neil plunged into work; he thought the *Freedom's* office must be the busiest place in the village. "The work is sure piled up, Miss Van Vliet."

Busy clipping and pasting dummy sheets, she agreed. "If we're going to get next week's edition out on time, we will have to have some help on Tuesday. Do you know a boy you might ask?"

"Yes, ma'am. I can get Clay."

"Of course."

"I can ask on my way home."

There was a slender red-and-white pole outside the barbershop. Neil had been inside the day he picked up the pie tin. He remembered the shining battery of brass

39

cuspidors. With the fragrance and the fancy shaving mugs, the shop seemed like a club that would be fun to join. Clay was waiting near the back of the shop, as usual.

"Hey, Clay! Miss Van Vliet wants you to work next Tuesday."

Clay smiled, "Sure."

When Tuesday arrived, Neil came early to work, but everyone else was there before him. Miss Van Vliet had mixed the ink and Mr. Rogers had already pulled proofs.

While Neil went to the post office, Clay kept the stoves fired up so that the ink could flow properly. Later Mr. Rogers showed Neil how to seize the press handle with both hands and pull it toward him, leaning back to gain the advantage of his weight.

"This is called the devil's tail—and when you've manned it, you can properly be called a printer's devil."

Neil pulled the bar and Clay kept his hands clean so that he could lift the sheets off carefully, as they were printed, hanging them on a line to dry. They all worked as a team and both boys were proud; Neil felt like a full-fledged member of the printing fraternity. At noon Clay went home to eat and beckoned Neil outside.

"My pa says not to take any pay from Miss Van Vliet."

"Why not? She won't ask you again if you don't take pay."

Clay shrugged. Finally Neil suggested, "Why don't you tell Miss Van Vliet what your father said—she'll know what to do."

Neil went back in to eat with Mr. Rogers. "I don't know how you learned all that in four years, sir. And I don't know how you learned all the words, either. When you have only a little room on a line you always think of a word to fit. I don't think I could do that."

"Mostly, Neil, you read. I love reading and I like words."

"I'll just have to read more then, because I've decided that I want to be like you and learn to set type."

"Hmm." Mr. Roger's reply sounded a bit questioning, Neil thought. From his pocket Neil produced an editorial clipped from Mr. Cook's paper. "Did you read this last week, sir?"

No trade sends into the world smarter, more active men than that of printing. One of the greatest lawyers England ever produced was a printer. The Lord Mayor of London is a printer. The Mayors of Glasgow, Edinburgh, and Perth and the Mayors of New York, Washington, and Savannah are printers. The recent Mayor of Boston was a printer. A dozen printers are in Congress. Stick to your business and peruse useful books. Cultivate your mind, contract no bad habits. Think of Franklin.

"That's interesting, Neil. I missed it, but I read one in the *Louisville Courier* that said, 'Our readers will have to excuse us for the non-appearance of several interesting pieces of news this morning—our compositors all being drunk.'"

Neil grinned and Mr. Rogers chuckled, patting him on the shoulder. "I'm glad to hear you want to be a printer. Printing is the art preservative of all the other arts."

After chores, Uncle Bert came for Neil and stayed to help fold papers so that Miss Van Vliet could address them, ready for Wednesday's delivery. When they finished she marked the accomplishment. "We've managed to do it again!"

From then on, Uncle Bert appeared each Tuesday night to help with the folding. On the way home Neil generally talked of the wonders of the newspaper business. One night they paused, coming from the barn, and Neil realized that he had done all the talking; he was discomfited until he felt Uncle Bert's hand on his shoulder. A frog quavered in the marsh.

Uncle Bert noted, "Now that's the first frog I've heard, Neil. The weather must have made up its mind to be spring." He said it as though he had impressed the day with a stamp of approval that admitted it into the real world. They walked toward the kitchen door and Neil felt that he was getting back into step with Uncle Bert's world.

Neil was bewildered—Uncle Bert seemed always at ease, whether at home on the farm or in the village. He was just himself. Neil felt as though he were two or three different people. At his own home on the farm, he had been one person. At Uncle Bert's farm he felt like a different person, and he felt still different in the village.

Of course, it was different in the village. Life moved faster there and he moved faster with it. Even crossing the street was lively, especially when the weather was good. Then he had to dodge between the many teams of oxen. But just as he managed to adapt to the life in the village it was time to return to the quiet of the farm. He felt always as if he were making a journey without quite knowing the direction to take.

The next morning, however, Neil knew he was back in his own real world when he glanced out the window of the office as he packed his delivery bag. Fats stood there making faces at him, waiting for him to come out. When Miss Van Vliet passed the window, Fats moved away.

"Who is that boy, Neil?"

"That's Fats Gunn, ma'am."

"Did you say Gunn?"

Neil nodded.

"Does he ever bother you?"

"I try to steer clear of him."

Miss Van Vliet crossed to her desk and then turned. "Why don't you ask Clay to help with the delivering? Two of you will make better time."

Neil happily agreed; he and Clay had not found time lately for their hikes by the river. He stopped next door to leave a copy of the paper for Ancel Hawkins.

"Morning, Cornelius, I'll trade a penny for that paper."

Neil was astounded, but he caught the penny. "Thanks, Mr. Hawkins, but you needn't!"

Neil crossed the street to pick up Clay.

"Clay, did you tell Miss Van Vliet what your father said?"

Clay nodded. "She gave Pa a note. Said I had to take pay same as you."

"See, I told you! She wants you to help deliver. Go ask—I'll wait."

It was a short wait. Clay came bounding out and the boys set off for Alexander's Livery and Feed Stable near the Triangle. Inside the door, next to the advertisements for Kitchell's Liniment and Kendall's Spavin Cure, was a sign that Neil liked and read aloud:

Whip light,
Drive slow,
Pay cash
Before you go!

After a printing office, Neil ranked a livery stable as an engrossing spot to visit. The rickety lean-to at the back was floored with wide spaces so that the water could dribble through when the stable gyp sponged and sloshed the running gear of the rigs. After he greased the "exes" he gave the wheels an appraising spin to be sure they ran free. Mr. Alexander's gyp was a perfectionist.

The barn was built along the side hill. A ramp, cleated with lengths of old fire hose, led down to the horses nickering in their stalls. As the boys came in they could hear Mr. Alexander bellowing to the swipe on duty with his pitchfork, "Hey, down there! Fetch up Star!"

Mr. Alexander turned and saw the boys. "Looks like I've got me some helpers. Ready to buckle a bellyband today?"

With regret Neil said, "Not today, Mr. Alexander. We're delivering for Miss Van Vliet."

One of the loafers stopped his whittling. "What you taking that slave paper for?"

"I ain't in business for my health," Mr. Alexander said quietly. "I advertise everywhere and if abolitionists want to rent my rigs that's fine with me."

Outside again, Neil said, "I like Mr. Alexander. Uncle Bert said he treats his horses good; he won't let anyone run 'em hard. Hey, Clay, on the way back, let's stop at Woodruff's and get some maple sugar with Mr. Ancel's penny."

"Mr. Ancel wouldn't like it if he knew he was paying for me."

"Why, Clay? He's always nice to me."

"You white. He told me stay on my own side the street."

Neil knew Clay was telling the truth; it puzzled and worried him into silence. They stopped next at Esau Shepherd's carpenter shop beside the saloon. Esau's shop was an orderly place; all the walls were lined with adzes, saws, hammers, awls, bits and braces, gauges, and planes of every size, each in its assigned space. The floor was swept; all the curly shavings were in one box beneath a large press.

The boys went through to the back, threading their way through the stacks of wood, breathing in their spices, guided by Esau's singing.

"Mr. Shepherd doesn't have time to do much carpentry work," Uncle Bert had told Neil, "because he's so good at making wheels. If Esau makes a wheel it gets stronger the older it gets. No one knows his secret. You can use the same woods—gum for the hub, ash for the spokes, beech for the axles, hickory for the

45

felly—but your wheel won't work the way his will. Maybe it's in the seasoning."

That's where the boys found Esau, at the wheelwright's bench. Clay gave him the paper and asked, "Mr. Shepherd, can I show Neil your hearse?"

Esau nodded and smiled. Neil noticed the paper was looked at quickly, and then put away. He wondered if Mr. Shepherd could read. At the far end of the building, he saw the hearse. He thought he had never seen anything so beautiful as that black carriage with its glass sides and black plumes on each corner.

"Just knowing you'd be riding in that would take the sting out of dying, wouldn't it, Clay?"

When they returned, Neil asked, "Sir, where did you learn to make a carriage like that?"

Esau took off his old hat and rubbed his grizzled head. "In the times of tribulation, son, in the times of tribulation. How's Miss Van Vliet?"

"She's working hard, sir."

"She's fine lady; first white person ever called me mister."

Esau continued singing and the boys went out and up the hill. Neil turned to Clay and asked, "Can you read?"

Clay shook his head.

"Can you write your name?"

Again Clay shook his head.

Neil stopped and said earnestly, "Look, Clay, you can learn. You have to. If I had a slate I'd show you, but I'll make sounds now. When we get back I'll print the sounds."

Clay listened as Neil explained, "We're going *up* this hill. That will be the first word you'll learn."

Neil searched the paper for large letters. "See, here's a *u* and here's a *p*. Put 'em together and they spell *up* and that's what we're doing, going *up* the hill. Now let's hear you make those sounds."

When Neil was satisfied, he said, "Turn that *u* on its side and you have a *c*—the first letter in your name." He stopped again, searching the paper for a *c*. "Now with that letter you can go two ways. You can make a hard sound or a soft sound."

Throughout the deliveries Clay practiced the sounds. Toward noon, on the way down Main Street hill, Neil pointed to the jeweler's sign. "See LaPierre? The first letter in his name is an *l*—the same letter your name has. When we get back I'll show you two words—*up* and *Clay*. Every day we'll learn two words."

Clay listened intently. Then, pointing to LaPierre's sign, he said, "There's a *p!*"

Neil laughed, "Hey, Clay, that's good. You get an *A* today!"

As Neil and Clay neared Front Street two boys lunged out at them from the corner, chanting, "Nigger lover! Dirty abolitionist!" They were gone as quickly as they had appeared. Neil jumped, recognizing neither of them. When he turned to ask Clay who they were, he found Clay also had disappeared!

Neil turned into the alley and the thought struck him. "I'll bet Fats steered them onto us—he knows I come back at noon!"

He could hear the stage, with Jack blowing the

horn, half a mile away, coming out of the Thick Woods, and knew it was time to eat.

At the livery stable a passenger alighted from the stage. He was a huge man with a short, black beard under a broadbrimmed hat, and he made his way to the office of the *Star of Freedom.*

Miss Van Vliet saw the man coming and went to the door to greet him. "Come in, Brother Levi! It's good to see you. Come out to the pressroom."

After an affectionate greeting with Mr. Rogers, Brother Levi turned to Neil to be introduced. Neil thought he had never seen a more serene man. Since Mr. Rogers also seemed serene to Neil, he thought it might simply be that there was so much more of Brother Levi, especially his nose.

"Young lady, I came all the way to Niles this morning for two reasons. One is to tell you how proud I am of you and your paper. I read every word in it and then I pass it around. And I brought an ad for seeds."

It was a long list; Neil thought it would require nearly half a page.

"If you can look this over and tell me what I owe, I'd like to settle up today."

Mr. Rogers pulled up a chair for Brother Levi.

"Thanks, Bill. A Niles man sat across from me on the stage this morning—talked nonstop all the way from Berrien."

"Who was he?"

"Someone called him Will. He said, 'If any more niggers flood the country I'm moving west. Niles is flooded with them.' I asked how many constituted a flood and Will said, 'There must be forty, and that's a flood.'"

"Considering Niles has twelve hundred people," Mr. Rogers said, "scarcely a flood."

"He asked me if I was a woolly. I said, 'I'm an abolitionist, as a Christian I have no other choice.'"

"That stopped him?"

"No. He thought a minute and then said, 'Well, I'm a Christian!' I said, 'In that case you will obey the biblical command to hide the outcasts and betray not him that wandereth. As I stepped down I whispered to him, 'Thou shalt not steal slaves from Africa!'"

Mr. Rogers slapped his knee and laughed. "Probably thought you were a minister. Maybe more abolitionists should take to stagecoach travel. How's the road?"

"About the same. Riding in Jack's coach is like being seasick on dry land." Brother Levi turned to Neil. "Cornelius, why don't you come with me for some lunch? I don't fancy eating alone."

Miss Van Vliet smiled her assent, and Neil went in great anticipation to the large brick building that was the American Hotel. He looked with dismay, however, at the long listing of dishes on the menu.

"I'll just get whatever you're going to have, sir."

After ordering, Brother Levi suddenly leaned toward Neil, saying urgently, "Change places, Cornelius."

Neil quickly moved so that he faced the door.

"See that man coming in, brown suit, smoking a cigar? Is he talking to anyone?"

"Only the waiter, sir. He's sitting down by himself."

"That's Sam Gunn, the slave stealer. Let me know if anyone comes to talk to him."

"I know a boy named Gunn—maybe they're related?"

"If he's mean, I'd say the chances are excellent. Sam Gunn's so mean he'd steal acorns from a blind hog. I'm surprised he's back in Niles."

"Was he here before, sir?"

"Yes, and got run out for inveigling a free slave off the steamer *Algoma*. He must be after more since the price is up."

Neil watched Sam Gunn and decided that he had never seen a quieter man, his every movement controlled. Not until Sam Gunn left the dining room did they return to the office.

Immediately Brother Levi said, "We saw Sam Gunn at the hotel."

After a long pause, Miss Van Vliet said, "That's interesting."

"Be careful."

"I will."

"Remember that our seed wagons will be going South as soon as the roads dry up. We'll be glad to help with any deliveries you may have."

Neil noticed the barest hesitation before Miss Van Vliet looked over at the tall case clock ticking away at the end of the room.

"Thank you, I believe I will send this clock back to my aunt in Virginia. I should have sent it long ago."

As Neil packed papers for the afternoon delivery, Miss Van Vliet said, "You heard Brother Levi tell me to be careful, Neil? I must give you the same warning. Sam Gunn never travels alone. Watch for any strangers when you are delivering and watch your speech. Please report anything suspicious to me, for I feel responsible for you."

"Don't worry, Miss Van Vliet. I'll be careful."

"When you leave Dr. Finley's paper and Mr. Comley's at the mill, will you tell them, quietly, that you've seen Sam Gunn?"

Neil nodded and went on to the barbershop for Clay. He found Clay's family was already aware of Gunn's return. Clay refused to go delivering. "Sam Gunn got too many men around." Clay didn't add, "I'm afraid." There was no need. Fear walked through his eyes.

"When you go deliver, Neil, watch out behind."

All the way to the mill the air was filled with the mellow thunder from the log-banking grounds along the river. As Neil climbed the mill stairs he watched the rafters prying the huge logs loose from their high piles and sending them crashing down the slope into the water. He waited until Joshua Comley finished pouring grain into the hopper.

"Miss Van Vliet said to tell you Sam Gunn is here."

The smile left Joshua's face.

"I saw him, eating at the American Hotel."

Without a word Joshua patted Neil on the shoulder and put the paper in an empty four sack. Dr. Finley's wife received the news as seriously and Neil went on to Mrs. Waldie's boarding house at the top of Sycamore Street hill. She asked him to step into the kitchen.

"Young man, you tell Miss Van Vliet that I think we have enemies. I found a sign tacked to my door that said, 'Nigger worshiper.' That was last week after you delivered the paper. No telling what'll happen tonight. I'll keep my eye out."

Neil reported this when he returned to the office. Miss Van Vliet looked at him, saying nothing. He thought she hadn't heard and began repeating the story. She thanked him then and went to tell Mr. Rogers.

Neil hung his bag in the back room and as he came through the pressroom Mr. Rogers beckoned to him. "You must be careful, Neil. Don't be afraid to talk to your uncle and aunt about all that you see or hear."

That night Neil changed his route going home, cutting through the woods. During supper he told about the day's events in order. "Uncle Bert, did you ever hear of Brother Levi from Berrien?"

"He's a Shaker—from Shaker Farm."

"What's a Shaker?"

Aunt Annie said, "They're thrifty, good folk, even if they don't believe in marriage."

Uncle Bert added, "Brother Levi grows seeds; has a huge barn and seed warehouse. Hires close to fifty men."

"They believe good spirits will not live where there is dirt, and I say they're right," Aunt Annie said.

Neil still didn't feel that he knew what a Shaker was, but he could see why Aunt Annie approved of them—his mother always said her sister was "nasty clean."

"Brother Levi took me to eat at the American Hotel."

"Land sakes! How did that happen?"

"He came to put an ad in the paper and he said he didn't like to eat alone."

52

"I declare! What did you have to eat?" Aunt Annie asked.

"Corn chowder and cabbage salad and rolls and little pieces of butter and hot gingerbread with whipped cream and napkins folded fancy in the glasses. Then the waiter put ice in the glasses and water."

"How much did it cost?" Aunt Annie asked.

"I don't know. Sam Gunn was eating there, too."

"Sam Gunn!" Uncle Bert put down his knife with honey on it.

"Wasn't he in that fracas at Berrien?" Aunt Annie asked.

Uncle Bert nodded. "He got a cook off the *Algoma* and took him as far as La Porte before the posse caught him. Sam was on horseback and he had the cook roped and running behind."

"A posse?" Now it was Neil's turn to ask, "What happened?"

"Sam Gunn got away. Leastways, he wasn't brought to trial."

Neil told them then about the sign on Mrs. Waldie's door.

In his deliberate way, Uncle Bert asked, "Did you tell Miss Van Vliet?"

Neil nodded and Uncle Bert warned, "It's not too soon for you to learn not to talk to anyone about what's happening. Talk's cheap till you want to buy it back. You remember that."

Aunt Annie, looking troubled, gathered the dishes. She dipped water and asked, "What Shakespeare quotation has Miss Van Vliet put in the paper this week?"

Uncle Bert read:

> Take the instant way;
> For honour travels in a strait so narrow
> Where one but goes abreast.

"Read on, Bert."

"Miss Van Vliet has an answer to Mr. Cook's article last week where he said he was against political abolitionism."

Aunt Annie stopped washing dishes to listen.

> Our neighbor of the *Republican* declares himself opposed to slavery, opposed to political abolitionism and in favor of annexation. We should be glad to know what kind of abolition he is in favor of, and whether he did not once oppose the scheme of annexation.

"She's right. There's only one kind of abolition and that's abolishing slavery!" Aunt Annie was pleased. "It's shameful that Mr. Cook has changed his mind and is for bringing Texas in as a slave state."

Neil said, "All the papers from the East are against Texas coming in as a slave state. The *Boston Post* said we might as well dissolve the Union the moment Texas is annexed."

"But," Uncle Bert reminded him, "there are more representatives and more senators from the South than there are newspapers and that is what will tell the tale. And if those Southern congressmen get to carve Texas up into four states they'll have even more men to send to Washington to vote for slavery."

This thought silenced them all.

After a time Neil asked, "Aunt Annie, why can't free colored boys go to school?"

Aunt Annie stopped cleaning the stove.

"It isn't right, is it?" Neil continued.

"No, I guess not, Neil," Aunt Annie said slowly. "It stands to reason they ought!"

That night Neil had so much to think about that he was sure he would be a long time getting to sleep. Instead, in the dark, the sad song Esau Shepherd sang at the wheelwright's bench came back to him:

> You go brute me, you go scorn me,
> You go scandalize my name,
> Since my soul got a seat up in the Kingdom,
> That's all right.

Somehow, it helped him to sleep.

4

O, Ye Peaceful Sabbath!

True to his promise, Mr. Rogers showed Neil how to set type. Neil was grateful that Mr. Rogers told him what to do and then walked away, for he felt as if he were all thumbs.

By lunchtime Neil had finished setting the legal notice and checked anxiously for any river of space running vertically through it before he showed it to Mr. Rogers.

"When do you think I can set more type, sir?"

"Well, now, maybe we could call Friday afternoon typesetting time. Providing all the delivering gets done by Thursday."

"I know I ask lots of questions, sir. I hope you don't get tired of them?"

"Bear in mind the answers may not always be right, Neil. What's on your mind?"

"I still don't understand about the Shakers except that Brother Levi grows seeds and sells them, and that they don't believe in getting married."

"That marriage rule is bound to put them out of business someday. They raise the best seeds in the country and make the best medicines. They're hard workers and everything they put a hand to works better

57

than anyone else's, whether it's a chair or a machine. They're especially thoughtful of women and children. For that reason alone, Brother Levi would have placed his seed ad in the *Star of Freedom*—even if he didn't oppose slavery. And he enjoyed taking you to eat."

"Uncle Bert said they got a posse after Sam Gunn last time he was here."

"True, Brother Levi organized the posse."

"Brother Levi!"

"With his helpers at the seed farm."

"I guess he was right about Sam Gunn being after free slaves, because Clay is scared to go delivering. He said Fats is Sam Gunn's nephew."

"Where does Fats live?"

"On Water Street."

"That's interesting. You can't get much closer to the river than that."

Mr. Rogers puffed on his pipe awhile. "Sam Gunn lives on the water, too, but on a grander scale. Brother Levi saw it—he said Sam lives on an island in the Ohio River in a great mansion. An avenue leading to it is lined with sycamore trees. You can see why Sam Gunn is dead serious about slave stealing. It takes money to keep such an estate, as well as slaves."

Mr. Rogers and Neil returned to work and printed election notices. As Neil was getting ready to take them to the recorder's office, Miss Van Vliet came out to the pressroom, chuckling. "Did you read Mr. Cook's piece in the *Republican?* It may not win him many friends among the young ladies of this village." She read to them:

Winter Is Gone

We have had only one big snow, the thermometer
hardly below freezing. Oh for an old fashioned New
England winter when the snowbanks were up to the
eaves. . . . These Michigan winters may go to grass and
we will talk about what used to be . . . when winter
was winter and girls were plenty and none of your
starched up, puny, pale, sickly, nipping parlor orna-
ments such as may be seen at the present day, but real
plump, rosy cheeked, hale and hearty unassuming
maids such as tore the heart of a young man all to
slivers. . . .

Neil smiled, but felt, somehow, aloof from the others'
laughter. He went out into the soft air. Spring brought
no thoughts of girls to Neil, except for his sisters. Ever
since his mother's letter had come he'd been thinking
of them. His father, she said, was up and about and
Millie had the fever now. She hoped that little Ada
would escape and that she would, too.

Neil thought also of Shep. "I hope there won't be
any lightning or thunder storms. That's when Shep
needs someone."

Everywhere the thin green lines of spring advanced,
the birds were streaming north, and Neil felt somehow
adrift.

"Would it be all right," he asked at supper, "if I built
a trap to catch a rabbit for a pet?"

"So long as you put him in a pen," Uncle Bert
said.

"I could move the pen around the yard, and then he

would keep the grass cut down." Aunt Annie's eyebrows lifted in doubt.

"Did you ever make a rabbit trap, Uncle Bert?"

"Yes. I guess I recollect how to do that."

After Friday's work Neil took every short cut he could so as to get home and start work on the trap. He had to wait, though, sitting quietly till Uncle Bert finished milking Amy, the brindle cow. Waiting was not unpleasant, for he liked listening to Uncle Bert's singing.

"Amy likes it quiet," Uncle Bert reasoned, "so she can hear her song. Then she gives down more milk."

Neil leaned back, stroking the barn cat as she lapped her milk, watching the dust motes filter through the late afternoon light. The steady swish of the milk into the pail made a harmony of tenor notes to Uncle Bert's baritone.

Milking was restful here, Neil thought. At home, he sometimes hid in the corncrib to escape his pa's angry beating of the cows with the milking stool. Afterward, his stomach took a time unwinding. "Why," Neil wondered, "can't Pa go at life like Uncle Bert does?"

Nothing ever fazed Uncle Bert; he worked ahead of the seasons the way Aunt Annie worked ahead of the clock. He seemed to be playing a game with the weather, never allowing it to catch him out. He was always ready for sugaring as soon as the weather turned. His fences were ready when it was time to turn the cows out to pasture. No matter what the weather did, Uncle Bert would outwit it and have his haying done by a certain day and his oats cut by another.

Uncle Bert interrupted Neil's musing. "You take this

milk up to the house while I look for some boards for the trap. We want seasoned wood. If we use new wood, the rabbit won't come in."

By the time Neil returned, Uncle Bert had cut a hole, large enough for a rabbit, in a long board. They measured and sawed and nailed until time for supper.

Uncle Bert explained, "Tomorrow we'll fasten the cord to this long piece, run it down inside, and tie it to the bait. When the rabbit eats the bait, the cord will release this piece to drop down and block the hole. We'll have to groove it."

They finished the trap after supper on Saturday. Neil tied the cord around a carrot; he scattered a little wheat, too.

"Uncle Bert, if there's a rabbit in the trap tomorrow I'll have to fix a place for him right away."

"If you have a rabbit you'd best put him in the shed. Your aunt isn't going to stand for anyone making a hutch on Sunday."

Neil came into the kitchen and found his bathwater ready in the tin tub. All the while he was washing he worried that he should have put a larger carrrot in the trap. Aunt Annie came to inspect.

"I declare, Neil, I don't know what you think you've been doing. Look at this dirt under your ears and down your neck!" She soaped the cloth and found each nook and cranny she claimed he'd missed. He dried himself, surprised he had any skin left at all.

His last thought before sleep came was about the rabbit. "Dear God, please let there be a rabbit in the trap tomorrow."

His first thought in the morning came the instant he opened his eyes. "Rabbit! Be there!"

Neil dressed hurriedly, and made his bed in one-half a minute. He ran outdoors. No rabbit! The bait was not touched. Neil was thunderstruck. He went on to the barn. "Uncle Bert, no rabbit even came near, and I've seen 'em every night around here!"

"I'm not surprised, you scarcely ever catch one the first day. Be patient, stay out of the yard, and you'll likely find one has ventured in by this time tomorrow." Uncle Bert grinned. "You think a few prayers in church this morning might turn the trick?"

Neil didn't mention that he had tried prayer and found it wanting. He waited for Uncle Bert and walked with him to the house for breakfast. Afterward, when Aunt Annie pronounced everything "set to rights," they were free to leave in the newly washed and polished buggy. She complimented Neil on the good job he had done in polishing the harness.

As they approached the church, Neil could hear the horn being blown to assemble the people. He wished he could blow it; he loved its clear tone. He remembered Aunt Annie telling about Sabbath morning in the schoolhouse, years before the present church was built. That morning the sound of a horn announced the approach of a keelboat.

"All the men of the congregation," Aunt Annie said, "with one exception, seized their hats and hurried down to the river to welcome it." Neil figured the exception had been Uncle Bert.

That wouldn't happen this morning, he thought wistfully. Mr. Lord's church was further from the river.

With the church doors closed no one would hear the keelboat's horn.

People were coming from all directions, on foot, in farm wagons, in buggies, talking quietly; the day belonged to the church. Neil helped Aunt Annie down and then helped Mrs. Finley, since she and the doctor drove up at the same time. He rode around back with Uncle Bert to tie Bessie to the rail outside the barn.

"Good morning, Margaret," Aunt Annie said, pleased to have this time for a visit. Neil was happy to see Dr. Finley. "Everyone," he thought, "is glad to see Dr. Finley." The seating committee always assigned Dr. Finley the first pew below the pulpit after Mr. and Mrs. Bacon's pew; no one felt slighted over the choice.

When the pew doors were closed, the Reverend Lord entered and ascended the stair leading to the pulpit. The young women in the choir looked up with rapt attention.

"This church," Aunt Annie sniffed, "has more single women than any other in Niles, all out to snare Mr. Lord. Pity he's so handsome. A poor reason to go to church, if you ask me."

Neil liked listening to Mr. Lord preach because he left r's out of lots of words and added an r at the end of other words. Suddenly, when Mr. Lord mentioned the word *water* (pronouncing it "wattah"), Neil was stricken. He had forgotten to dump the pail of slops to the pigs! Aunt Annie had told him not to forget, and she had put the pail next to the door of the summer kitchen. Boy! He'd do that the minute he got home—before she noticed.

Afterward, as they filed out to shake Mr. Lord's hand, Neil drifted away to the end of the vestibule. He overheard one woman say, "Look at them—all those abolitionists get together, don't they? Well, we'll see how they like paying Mr. Lord's salary when we leave!"

On the way home Neil observed, "Mr. Lord doesn't talk the way we do. He sounds different."

"Mr. Lord talks that way because he's from Maine," Aunt Annie explained. "Mrs. Nathaniel Bacon is his sister; she talks the same."

"I guess," Uncle Bert said, "that the man in the next pew didn't like the prayer ending. He was standing with the rest until Mr. Lord said, 'Let us remember those in bondage, as bound with them.' Then he sat down real quick. I thought a thundercloud had come over his face."

"I shall tell Mr. Lord I was proud of that prayer," Aunt Annie declared. "He said he would try to stop by later this afternoon."

When Neil told of the conversation he had overheard, Uncle Bert was astounded. "Who did you say was leaving?"

"Neil's right, Bert. Mrs. Bacon told me that twenty-one are withdrawing in protest. They have already asked for letters of dismission."

"Twenty-one! What are they protesting?"

"They say they do not believe in immediate abolition. They believe in moderation and do not subscribe to separating a man from his property."

They rode home in troubled silence. Uncle Bert was figuring how much money the church would be losing;

Aunt Annie was wondering how much they could increase their giving; Neil was thinking he could ask Mr. Rogers to come to church and that Aunt Annie would ask him home to dinner and then he wouldn't have to eat Lutie's cooking on Sunday.

When Uncle Bert paused at the side door to let Aunt Annie step down, Neil hurried to check the rabbit trap. The trap door was closed! He was so excited he thought he would never reach the shed without dropping the trap. He tried to lift the board, but it wouldn't budge. Carrying the trap into the kitchen, he put it on a chair.

"Uncle Bert, this board is stuck. I can't lift it!"

"It's likely warped from the dew. I'll just give it a start." Uncle Bert pulled hard. Suddenly the board lifted free and the rabbit, with a great leap, landed right in the bucket of slops! The slops went splashing all over the floor as the frightened rabbit hopped out, upsetting the bucket, and ran wildly around the kitchen, in and out of the buttery, and into the sitting room.

"Sakes alive!" Aunt Annie shrieked. "Get that rabbit, he's going every which way!"

They tried, they all tried, running through the sitting room, clear through to Neil's bedroom.

"Bert, close that upstairs door!"

Neil heard the door slam as he dived under the bed in his room. He was too late. He had only a glimpse of Aunt Annie's skirt and Uncle Bert's legs and the rabbit colliding violently in the doorway. Then Neil slithered out, closing the door behind him.

"Bert, close our bedroom door!"

She called too late; the rabbit had jumped into the

wardrobe where Aunt Annie had put her hat. She banged the door shut.

"Now," she faced them both, "when I open this door, I want that rabbit caught."

They knew she meant it.

"All right, Annie. All right. Open the door," Uncle Bert said.

The rabbit tore out the moment the door swung back and Neil fell upon it, dripping wet, slippery, its heart beating wildly against his chest. He held it firmly and walked out the back door. Feeling the frightened beating of that heart, Neil knew he could never be happy caging this rabbit. Even so, he stood for a moment, torn.

"I guess this rabbit couldn't take the place of Shep, after all." Neil walked to the field beyond the corncrib. Gently, he put the rabbit on the ground. In two bounds it was away in the brush; Neil wished the ache in his throat would go as quickly.

"Neil," Aunt Annie called, "you take what's left of those slops out right now and then you can help me clean this floor. Land sakes! What a way to spend the day. There'll be no dinner till this house is put right."

Neil carried the bucket out and dumped the few remaining slops over the fence into the pigs' trough.

"If that had happened at home," he thought, "my mother would have laughed, like as not."

"I declare, Bert, you ought to have had more sense," Aunt Annie said as she wiped up the floor.

"Well, Annie, it's done now. What do you want me to do?"

"Sponge off Neil's suit—slops all over it!"

Neil stood patiently as Uncle Bert took a damp cloth to his suit and shoes.

"Does he smell?" Aunt Annie asked.

"Smells all right to me."

"I'll air the suit tomorrow; now you both change your clothes, and then we'll get after the floors."

By half past three all the floors were clean, every wet spot the bedraggled rabbit had trailed after him had been wiped up, every stray potato peeling had been found.

"Now we can think of getting dinner on the table," and Aunt Annie glanced out the kitchen window.

"Land sakes, there's Mr. Lord driving in. Go welcome him, Bert, while I get out of this apron."

They all went into the sitting room; Neil was quiet, praying his stomach would not make any rumbles. After a while Aunt Annie excused herself. "We're going to have an early supper, Mr. Lord, and I'll be much put out if you don't enjoy it with us. It'll take no time at all—Neil can set table."

If the crust on the chicken was more crisp than usual, no one noticed. Mr. Lord was obviously enjoying himself, and when he recommended that Aunt Annie show his sister how to cook chicken, she accepted the compliment with a nod and a smile and refrained from mentioning wet rabbits.

Afterward Aunt Annie told Neil, "That's a terrible blow to Mr. Lord, losing twenty-one people. It was good he got to talk over his troubles with your Uncle Bert. All the churches are going through the same. I thought maybe the Presbyterians could be more understanding, but now it's happening to us, too. Sometimes I wonder if the country will hold together."

Neil sat quietly under the weight of the day.

"I'm sorry about the rabbit, Neil. Did you let him go because I was so provoked?"

"No, Aunt Annie. I just didn't want to keep him caged, after all. He was so scared. But I feel bad for all the work Uncle Bert went to, making the trap."

"Don't fret about that. Bert enjoys making things. And if the rabbit hadn't gotten loose and run all over the house we would have eaten that dinner and then what would I have offered Mr. Lord? As Mr. Shakespeare says, 'Ill blows the wind that profits nobody.'"

5

Wednesday's Child Is
Full of Woe

Clay watched for Neil the next morning and walked with him. He helped sort and pack the papers but still refused to go delivering. "Sam Gunn can sell anybody he catches."

"Clay! Nothing is going to happen in broad daylight!"

"Sam Gunn didn't wait for night to take that cook."

"All right, Clay, you work on your words and I'll knock when I come by."

Clay produced some white pine pitch to chew.

"Hey, Clay—where'd you get it?"

"Down to the tannery. Scraped it off some logs. Pa melted it down and strained it."

"Well, you went to the tannery, Clay, and nothing happened to you."

"Pa went, too." Clay paused. "I'm not the only one scared."

"Who else?"

"My uncle. He tans deer hides. He said Ancel Hawkins came walkin' around the tannery last week."

"Probably wanted to buy some leather, Clay."

"Ancel Hawkins got his own tannery. Then Sam Gunn came couple of days after."

Neil looked at Clay, thinking.

"My uncle's big and he's strong. And he's scared."

Chewing vigorously and thoughtfully, Neil crossed the street again to make his usual stop at the shoe shop. He protested the penny tip. "That makes your paper more expensive, Mr. Hawkins."

"But it assures quick delivery, Cornelius," Ancel laughed.

"I'd deliver it whether he tipped or not," Neil thought. "But it's nice of him."

Neil crossed the Triangle, thinking that maybe Ancel had been looking for a worker to hire for his own tannery. "It's hard to get men to do such dirty work. I should have told Clay that."

At the livery stable Mr. Alexander accepted the paper and took an envelope from his pocket. "Morning, young man. Here's the new ad, I've marked it to run for six months."

Neil thanked Mr. Alexander and considered returning to the office with the envelope. "I don't think this has anything to do with a new ad!" In the presence of the other men, however, he thought it would be well to make his normal trek up the hill. The gusty morning wind helped to lift him, but at the top he turned quickly over to Main Street hill and then down past Mr. LaPierre's.

Mr. LaPierre hailed him. "Come in, come in, Cornelius. Just the person I was hoping to see. Will you tell Miss Van Vliet that I had visitors last night? They painted 'Abolitionist' on my window. If you see the marshal, you can tell him to stop by.

"Could you do me a favor, son? When you deliver

Mr. Comley's paper would you give him this note? Give it to him. Not to anyone else. Just as well if no one saw you."

"Yes, sir."

"Here's a penny for your trouble."

"That's all right, sir. I'm going there anyway."

"Thank you, Cornelius."

Mr. LaPierre's smile drew him in and braced him up. "That's funny. I feel better when I don't take Mr. LaPierre's penny than I do when I take Ancel's."

Neil stopped at the office to deliver Mr. Alexander's note and the message from Mr. LaPierre. As he came down the steps the keelboat horn sounded. He hitched up his canvas bag and started running toward the river. Many others headed there to watch the beautiful precision of the polemen's parade. He heard one man say, "I wouldn't mind trying it downstream with the current, but the trip up is a killer."

Neil thought that no matter how tired the men were, they must be enjoying this last stage of the trip before such an appreciative audience. He didn't understand how people could know which boat was coming, but some were calling out, "Come on, *Swallow!*" The boat was well named, gliding through the water as gracefully as a bird in flight.

Watching the men walking downstream, pushing hard with their shoulders against the top of the poles and then running back for new positions, Neil wondered if they ever fell into the river.

The boat pulled in, and as Neil turned toward the mill a stone struck him hard, above the ankle. The pain was so sharp that he dropped to his knee, drawing in his breath, holding his ankle. When he was able to stand, he looked about. Though Fats was nowhere visible, Neil knew whose arm had done the throwing.

Neil limped gingerly to the mill and then up Sycamore Street hill to Dr. Finley's. Under cover of the paper Mrs. Finley gave him a note for Miss Van Vliet.

"I have one more stop, Mrs. Finley, and then I'll take it right back to the office."

Neil reflected on all that seemed to be happening as he crossed the street to the schoolhouse. He hailed his friends as they came out for recess; he felt proud that they would see him working, carrying his paper bag. The boys looked at him and then turned their backs and shunned him.

For a moment Neil stood in disbelief, his cheeks flushed and his insides so quiet he wondered if his heart had stopped. It seemed a long time before he could swallow. As quickly as his ankle allowed, he went up the hill, his jaws set.

"I know why they did that. It's because I'm working for Miss Van Vliet. Well, I'd rather work for her than go to school with them any day!"

Mrs. Waldie drew Neil into her kitchen. "Young man, you tell Miss Van Vliet that I did what I promised when you were here last Wednesday. I sat in the dark by my bedroom window for almost an hour. Nothing happened, so I went to bed. Then someone threw rotten eggs at my front door. I ran to the window and I saw a short person—seemed heavy—running back into the trees."

"Yes, ma'am, I'll tell her right away."

72

"And if you see the marshal, you tell him. Doubt much will come of it; he thinks chasing pigs is more important. But you tell him."

"Yes, ma'am, I will."

"You tell him six rotten eggs add up to one big stink!"

When Neil handed over Mrs. Finley's note and reported Mrs. Waldie's trouble, Miss Van Vliet asked him to tell Mr. Rogers.

"It is obvious," she said, "that there is an effort to frighten the subscribers. Mr. Alexander says he has had strange men loitering about all week. Mrs. Finley says their house was watched toward dusk and into the night. Mrs. Waldie has had trouble twice and now Mr. LaPierre has had his window painted."

Neil added, "Mrs. Waldie said she was sure whoever threw the eggs was short and heavy. I thought it could be Fats." Suddenly Neil remembered all those early deliveries when he thought someone was following him on the route—of course Fats knew each subscriber!

"We'll see what you turn up on your afternoon deliveries, Neil. Be careful," Mr. Rogers said.

They ate that noon in silence. Neil's ankle was beginning to pound and the shunning by his classmates had made a heaviness in his chest.

Finally Mr. Rogers took a doughnut from his box. He looked at it, weighed it, and thunked it on the edge of the table.

"Good food, Neil, is one of the joys of this world, and there ought to be a law to keep women like Lutie Bibbins from cooking. I swear you could sell these doughnuts to a furniture company for curtain rings!"

Neil smiled then. "Here, sir, have some of Aunt Annie's walnut cookies."

Neil's afternoon proved uneventful and he looked forward to his only westside delivery. He had to wait, though, to cross the bridge until a herd of oxen had clattered over. He enjoyed watching the drover's dog work. "I have to admit that dog is smarter, even, than Shep."

He walked to the brick house, high on the bluff, where the Misses Mansfield lived. They were gentle Quaker ladies. Always when he brought the paper they would ask, "Won't thee step in, son, for a cooky and a glass of milk?" Neil never refused. Today he told them he was worried, that some subscribers were finding names scrawled on windows.

"Thee must not concern thyself about us. Our guards will be alert."

"Your guards, ma'am?"

"Yes. Our pet skunks. I shall tie Ebenezer to the front porch tonight and Sister will tie Emmaline to the side porch. We thank thee for thy warning."

Neil grinned. He wondered how he could bear the wait to find how well the guards had worked. When he reported how the gentle Quakers were prepared to do battle, the tense day ended in laughter.

On Neil's way home, Clay, with his finger to his lips, met him at the rear of the barbershop. He pointed down Water Street, urging Neil along. Peering around the next corner Neil saw Fats crouching beside a window well with a small, slatted box. He was poking at something inside with a stick. Neil saw smoke and realized the stick was a match.

"What's he doing, Clay?"

"Burnin'."

"But what?"

"A mouse."

"A live mouse?"

Clay nodded. For a moment the boys looked at one another. Neil put his hand on his stomach. "He makes me sick. I'd like to burn him! I'm going home. You go in, too."

At supper Neil was quiet. Finally Aunt Annie asked about the day's events and Neil told about Mr. LaPierre's window and Mrs. Waldie's rotten eggs, and about the skunks. They laughed about the skunks and were disgusted over the scrawls and the eggs.

"I don't need help with these few dishes," Aunt Annie said. "You two take turns reading."

Uncle Bert opened the *Niles Republican* to read Mr. Cook's reply to Miss Van Vliet's earlier question.

Well then, we are in favor of the abolition of slavery and would have it done just when the slave states of themselves see proper to do it and not before. In regard to our being once opposed to annexation, we must confess that when we were a bachelor and smoked our segar in solitude, we strenuously opposed annexation for a long time. But a certain fair one crossed our path one sunny day and we changed our mind, and for four years we have been one of its strongest advocates and we cannot but express our astonishment when we see the maid of the 'Star' opposing annexation so strenuously.

"A slippery answer!" Aunt Annie sniffed.

Neil read from the council news: "The poll tax is $1.00 each year on every legal voter to be paid in money or eight hours work on streets and lanes and alleys."

"That's good news," Uncle Bert said. "Last year I worked ten hours."

Neil continued, "The sexton is to be paid $2.00 for digging graves for all over ten years of age and $1.25 for persons under ten years of age.

"Any person removing any ladders from the Engine House will be fined $5.00."

Uncle Bert let out a roar of laughter at this, and it was some time before he could explain.

"Job Brookfield is the reason council passed that. He was going past the engine house early one morning and saw a ladder leaning against the building. He thought, 'That's where my ladder went,' and he picked it up and walked home with it. The commissioner of the fire company was up on the roof, and he was stuck up there two hours hollering for the marshal."

"Will Mr. Brookfield have to pay a fine?"

"No, Neil, it was his ladder!" Uncle Bert folded his paper, chuckling. "Guess I'll bring in a little kindling, Annie."

Uncle Bert said this every night, even though he had brought in an armload of kindling at suppertime. What he really wanted was to look at the sky, to feel the air, and to smell the sweet nighttime scents.

To Uncle Bert the weather was like an errant child, something he must keep an eye on. Neil went along, and they stood next to the woodpile looking up at the moon.

76

"See those fuzzy horns on the moon, Neil? This time of year, that means a rain about four in the afternoon. Especially as the ground didn't have any dew last night. Good time to see that the chickens are shut up tight—the foxes will be out tonight. Now take a night when the dew's heavy—you never have to worry about foxes then—they don't like it."

In the woods below, as if he knew he were being talked about, a fox barked once, twice; two little owls softly wailed their questioning; frogs in the nearby pond gravely answered yes.

Uncle Bert and Neil stood listening. Then they picked up a little kindling and walked back to the house.

6

The Golden Day Ends

Neil had no need to wait to discover how well the skunks had protected the porches. As he neared Front Street the next morning, the air was redolent with skunk odor. He chuckled all the way to the office.

Miss Van Vliet met him at the door, laughing. "For the first time in my life, Neil, I'm happy about skunk smell. I doubt you'll see much of Fats this week."

"I think, ma'am, Fats must have met both Ebenezer and Emmaline!"

Mr. Rogers came in, drying his hands. "I've just finished washing the scrawls off our windows, Neil. In fact, I had a double dose—my rooming house was treated to a porch full of garbage last night."

Miss Van Vliet was provoked. "It is certainly odd that the marshal never seems to see any of this mischief! Especially when we're so close to the pound."

"He doesn't care about anything, ma'am. He said yesterday that he's quit, he's just waiting for the council to appoint a new marshal."

"That's good news, Neil! Perhaps we'll see a change around this village then."

Neil left for the post office, holding the door as

Ancel Hawkins entered with a large bunch of lilacs. "I thought these might reduce some of the skunk odor, Miss Van Vliet."

Through the window, Neil saw her bury her face in the heavy blooms and smile her thanks. He wondered, "Does he like Miss Van Vliet? Does she know how Ancel feels about Clay?"

Neil stopped to see Clay. "We got our windows painted last night."

"So did we."

"Lutie Bibbins had garbage thrown on her porch. Sounds like more than one person doing all that, doesn't it?"

Clay nodded and grinned, "'Cause one person was across the river meeting skunks." The boys dissolved into laughter until Clay produced a gristle ball from his pocket.

"It's from the nose of a big sturgeon. You can have it, I can get another one. It bounces real good."

"I'll trade you, Clay. When I go home, I'll get you some arrowheads. My mother collects them."

Neil went on to the post office without having to worry about Fats, but he was watchful of strangers anyway. When he returned to the office he emptied the mailbag and sorted the papers before he began clipping the articles that Miss Van Vliet had circled.

From the *Green Mountain Freeman:*

John C. Calhoun, the great apostle of slavery, is a ruling elder in the Presbyterian Church. Is it so?

Neil raised his eyebrows. "Wait till Aunt Annie reads this!"

From the *Savannah Republican,* March 23, 1845:

Slaves and Theology

This paper advertises a tract of land to be sold, also at the same time and place, the following negro slaves, to wit: Charles, Peggy, Antonett, Davy, September, Maria, Jenny and Isaac—levied on as the property of Henry T. Hall to satisfy a mortgage issued out of McIntosh Superior Court in favor of the Board of Directors of the Theological Seminary of the Synod of South Carolina and Georgia versus Henry Hall.

Neil thought, "Not just words—real people. I expect September was born in September!"

From the *Indiana Freeman:*

(Letter from a Presbyterian Minister in Lexington, Kentucky)

I hope the friends of humanity at the North will continue to speak on. They are exerting an influence here. Their action elicits talk, discussion and enquiry. It is because they speak and write that the subject is kept awake at the South. Speak on brethren, let your light shine—hold conventions, pass resolutions and scatter light. For the history of slavery is the history of ruin and desolation the world over. If ever the South is saved from the advancing ruin of slavery, the North will be, in one sense, her salvation by holding before the South her interest and conscience.

When Neil finished reading, his resolve matched Miss Van Vliet's. "I hate slavery and Sam Gunn's men can't scare me into changing my mind!"

Miss Van Vliet handed him a short item to be set; he read it on the way to the pressroom.

For the last five months the subject as to whether the Methodist Church is to be divided or not, has excited much interest in that body of Christians. It will be as slavery decides.

Mr. Rogers took this and handed Neil an envelope. "Would you run and give this to Mr. Jason? He just passed the window. Tell him I'd like two sacks of mushrooms."

Mr. Jason the mushroom man—no one seemed to know his full name—came to town every spring with huge morel mushrooms. He could find them when no one else could. Sometimes he came with catnip for tea, and if one hesitated about buying he would ask, "Ye want to live as long as I have, don't ye? Then drink catnip tea."

"And how old are you, Jason?" people would ask.

"I be eighty-one, come January," he would reply, finding a convenient place where he could sit, his basket over his knees, little bundles of catnip spread out on the step.

Everyone came to buy of the little man with the hunched back and the long white beard. Children sometimes brought broken toys, and from one of many pockets in his baggy overalls Mr. Jason would produce fine wire and small pliers and repair them.

"Mr. Jason," Neil called, "Mr. Rogers wants some mushrooms."

There was nothing wrong with Mr. Jason's hearing;

he turned about, waiting for Neil. Suddenly there was a yell: "Slavocrats and hunchbacks make good partners!"

Neil turned and saw that Fats had ventured as far as the corner after all. Mr. Jason heard only what he wished to hear and went on calmly, choosing the largest of his mushrooms. Only Neil was embarrassed.

When Neil returned with the mushrooms, Mr. Rogers gave him one of the sacks. "This is for your Aunt Annie—a thank-you for those good doughnuts she sent. This one is for Lutie Bibbins, though I don't know what she'll manage to do to them in the cooking."

"Aunt Annie will like these, sir. We've not had any yet."

Miss Van Vliet was on her knees, dusting shelves under the counter. "If you'll bring those boxes from the storeroom, Neil, we can put them here."

As they filled the shelves, working their way toward the end window, Neil saw the sunlight glinting on the medallion at her throat. "Miss Van Vliet, that's a penny on the ribbon around you neck!"

"Yes, it is. Can you see the figure on it?"

"It's a slave—isn't it?"

"Come over to the light." She unfastened the ribbon and showed Neil the words beneath the kneeling slave: "Am I not a Woman and Sister?" Beneath these words was the date, 1838.

"A very great Quaker lady, Lucretia Mott, gave that to me, and I treasure it." She looked at it carefully before fastening it on again. "I'll finish here while you and Mr. Rogers eat, Neil."

Because it was too beautiful a day to remain inside,

Neil and Mr. Rogers walked down to the water. The river, always busy, was especially so now when the fish were coming up from Lake Michigan to spawn. The water was so thick with fish that Neil could not see the bottom. Commercial fishermen were seining above the bridge, while others dipped their nets, depositing the fish in slat boxes at the edge of the water.

The arks were loading at the wharves before moving down river, while the *Davy Crocket,* steaming up the river, announced its arrival with a ding-donging bell. The big boat had an ornamental prow, half-alligator, half-horse, and the steam exhaust was piped so that it emerged from the monster's mouth. No boat on the river fascinated Neil so much as this.

"Better look while we eat, Neil."

Neil asked something then that had been worrying him. "Mr. Rogers, do you think Sam Gunn is trying to scare Miss Van Vliet out of printing the paper?"

Mr. Rogers thought a good while. "I don't know, Neil. He may be trying to keep his men busy, or he could be trying to frighten someone into talking."

"About slaves, sir?"

"I expect so, since that seems to be his unsavory business."

"Clay is more scared than ever. He says his uncle works at the tannery and he's scared, too. Sam Gun's been walking around there."

"Mr. Morton runs the tannery and I doubt that he'd let anything happen there, Neil."

Then Neil summoned his courage and talked of his own worry. "What did your father say, sir, when you decided to go to work?"

"My father was dead when I became an apprentice, Neil. My mother had married again, so it actually eased the situation."

"I don't think my father would like it if I said I wanted to work on a paper. I've two sisters and I'm the only one to help."

"I doubt you'd respect yourself if you didn't help. You're young. You have time. If you really want to be a printer, keep it in the back of your mind and keep reading as Mr. Cook advised in that editorial you showed me. The chance will come if you don't hurry it. Hurry breeds trouble, Neil."

For a time they watched the mud turtles slipping from the logs at the river's edge. Then Mr. Rogers got out his pipe and between puffs said, "Sometime, Neil, I want you to read one of Shakespeare's plays. You'll think this is an odd answer to your question—telling you to read a love story. But *Romeo and Juliet* isn't really a love story; it's a tragedy that came about because of hurry. The parents were overexcited and so were the children. Everything in it happens by blind chance. None of them could take life a day at a time; they had to hurry it—right into trouble. I'd hate that to happen to you, Neil."

Mr. Rogers stood up and stretched. "Now that I've advised against hurry, I think it would be well if we hurried back to work."

Neil grinned. They walked back to the office, leaving the sunlight, leaving the little green herons skimming the shore to lace the trees and river together.

Later, as the sky clouded over, Neil thought Uncle

Bert would be right in his weather prediction. But the clouds passed by, the sky grew extraordinarily light, and he thought, "Uncle Bert is wrong this time."

Then, at the very moment the case clock in the office struck four, large drops began coming down, the sky turned black, there was lightning and a great thunderclap.

Miss Van Vliet looked at Neil, standing in the office doorway. "Are you frightened, Neil?"

Neil shook his head slowly, in wonder. "No. Uncle Bert was right. He said it would rain at four o'clock today."

Miss Van Vliet laughed, and Mr. Rogers came to watch with them as the storm beat against the windows. It lasted thirty minutes, the water running high in the street, churning it to mud. Mr. Rogers had time to tell Neil a funny story about Mr. LaPierre before Uncle Bert came with an offer of a ride home. They closed a little early.

Aunt Annie fixed the mushrooms for supper, laughing as Neil told of the skunk smell, frowning as he recounted the stories about scrawls on the windows and the garbage on Lutie's porch.

"Lutie Bibbins will never put a handsome widower like Mr. Rogers out, no matter what Sam Gunn's men throw on her porch," she said.

Neil told of Mr. LaPierre's adventure, trying to tell the tale exactly as Mr. Rogers had.

"Ever since the window-painting episode, Mr. LaPierre had been especially alert and had noticed that his house was being watched. He was not sleeping as well as usual and thought quite often that he heard

86

strange noises in the night. He wasn't sure whether the noises were from squirrels on the roof, from the watchers turned prowlers, or from chicken thieves.

"He had lost some chickens to a thief recently, so when he heard a noise Tuesday night he got up. Not, as Mr. Rogers said, 'attired for the hunt, just wearing his one-piece nightshirt.'

"He took his shotgun and went out to see. His hound came up behind Mr. LaPierre and pressed his nose, which was quite cold, against Mr. LaPierre's bare leg. Mr. LaPierre let off both barrels of his gun and killed three chickens. So they gave a party and both Miss Van Vliet and Mr. Rogers were invited."

Uncle Bert and Aunt Annie laughed until Uncle Bert had to wipe his eyes.

After good work and good humor, Neil's orderly room and his clean bed came as a benediction to the golden day. Almost. He had just drifted into sleep when the wind-driven rain came spatting in, wetting the floor boards before he could get the window down. Usually he would be glad for the rain, glad for all the plants needing it; but getting back into bed and pulling the covers up over his shoulders, he found himself shivering with sudden dread.

"When," Neil thought, "is Sam Gunn going to leave Niles? When are his men going to leave? When will Clay and I ever deliver together again if they don't go?"

7

Toil and Trouble

The rain in the night was hard, bringing down a lot of dead wood. Before Neil left for work he picked up the litter; each time he passed the barberry bush a pair of brown thrashers hissed and squawked, warning him away from their nest.

Skirting the puddles on the way to the village, he thought of Mr. Roger's comment on hurry. "I hope Sam Gunn is hurrying into trouble."

Calm, however, prevailed until Wednesday when Neil began his deliveries. The taunting voice of Fats followed him up and down Main Street hill. "There goes the nigger lover!" Fats even followed him inside Clark's General Store, yelling, "Here comes the dirty abolitionist!"

Fats gave Neil a hard shove. Neil lost his balance and fell against a barrel that held a pile of sleigh bells. They came down with resounding tones.

Mr. Clark sprang toward the door. "Get out of here, Gunn. I don't want to see you around here again!"

Fats appeared stunned and left. Embarrassed, Neil apologized as he helped Mr. Clark pick up the bells.

Away from Main Street hill and Fats, Neil still found himself as shaken as if his boat had been caught in the

Devil's Whirlpool on the river. He was caught in Sam Gunn's wrath.

During the day five angry subscribers who had suffered painted windows or garbage asked that the paper be stopped. None felt obliged to pay any amount owing. At each cancellation a little spot in Neil's chest seemed to grow harder.

For the first time since the day of the big snow when he began work with such great hope, he had to admit that hope was shot through with holes.

In a gloomy mood, Neil trudged over to Sycamore Street hill to deliver Mrs. Waldie's paper. "At least Mrs. Waldie hasn't cancelled her subscription—even though everything bad happens to her first. Maybe this time she will escape."

She had not escaped. Mrs. Waldie took him through to the sitting room and pointed to the window. "Last night, someone threw a rock through this!"

For a moment he could scarcely summon the energy to comment. He could only shake his head in sympathy.

Mrs. Waldie was angry. "Won't do any good to talk to the marshal. I'm going to council tonight. Those men aren't going to like having a woman come talk to them, but that's too bad. I've got no man to do it for me."

When she heard Neil's report, Miss Van Vliet was outraged. "Scrawls and garbage are one thing; a broken window is quite another. That is destruction of property!"

Mr. Rogers agreed. "I'll go to council—perhaps I can help Mrs. Waldie; but it's not going to be easy to find rock throwers in the dark."

Neil noticed that while Mr. Rogers seemed very worried, Miss Van Vliet appeared extraordinarily calm. She busied herself composing a petition for the next issue. Later, when Neil told Aunt Annie and Uncle Bert about Mrs. Waldie's broken window, they were appalled.

"Just a matter of time," Uncle Bert warned, "and we can expect the same."

Neil determined to come home a different way each day and to be sure he was not followed. He didn't want any of Aunt Annie's windows broken.

After supper Uncle Bert opened the weekly edition of the *Star of Freedom* and read from the council minutes the results of the election at the schoolhouse.

Notices of the election held at the schoolhouse were posted by the Recorder at the American Hotel, the Pavilion, the Farmer's Inn, the Post Office, and the School House. Polls open 9:00 A.M. till 3:00 P.M.

Total votes cast: 174

Trustees elected: William Graves, Orson P. Willard, Nehemiah Dennis

President: Cogswell R. Green

Recorder: James Brown—151 votes
John Earl—1 vote

Pickpockets—1 vote
Negro Bill's dog—1 vote

Auntie Annie was outraged. "Women aren't considered bright enough to vote, but I can tell you no woman would waste votes like that!" She washed dishes in silence, outraged with the world of men.

After a quiet time, Uncle Bert thought to change the mood. "Here is your Shakespeare quotation, Annie:

> He that will have a cake out of the
> wheat, must needs tarry the grinding."

Aunt Annie listened and said nothing. She came to the table and sat down. She did not pick up her mending. She sat, her hands folded in her lap.

Uncle Bert and Neil were surprised into attentiveness.

Finally she asked quietly, each word heavy in the question, "What do you do after you've broken windows?"

"I suppose, Annie," Uncle Bert spoke as quietly, "that you could burn buildings, or hurt people, or find your slave, or be run out of the village as Sam Gunn was before."

"I'm beginning to worry about Neil."

"Why, Aunt Annie?"

"I would hate to think we had let you into danger."

"When I don't have my delivery bag they probably think I'm just another boy."

Uncle Bert said nothing, but he looked serious. They were silent. The ticking of the clock on the shelf vied with the metallic clinking of the cricket frogs.

"Even if Sam Gunn is run out," Aunt Annie said, "he will always come back for another slave and more mischief. We've no choice, Bert. Slavery must go, and we must do all we can to speed its going."

Gravely, Neil and Uncle Bert regarded one another.

Aunt Annie spoke decisively. "The way to change things is to hurt slave owners in their pocketbooks. Helping slaves escape is fine, but it doesn't hurt the owner enough, not when he can buy another slave. If people refused to buy cotton or sugar—we should use only free-labor goods, Bert."

"Where would we get them, Annie?"

"I've been reading about Southern farmers without slaves who sell free-grown cotton. And I read about a Quaker farmer in Mississippi who gins it and ships it out of Memphis by free labor on boats manned by free men."

"Where do they ship it?" Uncle Bert asked.

"I don't know, but the article said that Levi Coffin, in Indiana, is going to have a store for free-labor goods. That's closer. Maybe we could think about that."

"Miss Van Vliet might know more," Uncle Bert suggested.

The kitchen clock struck nine, vanquishing, for that moment, the frogs.

"Land sakes, Neil, time for bed!"

Neil climbed into bed thinking of Aunt Annie's determination to join in the fight against slavery. He went to sleep with great hope, since any cause that enlisted Aunt Annie must be a winning cause!

With Aunt Annie, the deed not only chased the thought, but lassoed it to a standstill. The next morning she sent Uncle Bert with Neil to ask Miss Van Vliet and Mr. Rogers to supper that night.

As he and his uncle turned out of Front Street, Neil

saw Mr. Rogers sweeping the path. "What's Mr. Rogers doing?"

Uncle Bert saw the jagged hole in the window. "Someone's thrown a rock!"

Inside, Miss Van Vliet was wiping the counter with a wet cloth. "Be careful, Neil, there is glass everywhere."

Neil brought a box from the storeroom and she threw the cloth into it. She seemed very calm; Neil knew her well enough now to be sure her mind was made up as to how to combat a trouble that the village law still seemed unwilling to notice.

She told Uncle Bert she'd love to come to supper. "I'll have to tell my landlady—she worries when I'm late."

Toward noon the bell of the approaching *Davy Crockett* could be heard through the hole in the window and Mr. Rogers suggested that Neil go ahead and eat. "I want to finish this window."

Neil went alone to the riverbank. A boy came down the plank of the boat and walked over to the log where Neil was sitting.

"You ride from Berrien?" Neil asked.

"From St. Joe. I'm second cook."

"Hey! You work on the *Davy Crockett?*"

"Cooking's not that much."

"How old are you?"

"Twelve."

"So am I. What's your name?"

"Francis Marion Ives."

"Are you related to the great Francis Marion, the Swamp Fox?"

94

"No," Francis laughed, "my pa heard a lot about him, I guess. Where do you work?"

"For a newspaper."

"What doing?"

"Delivering, cleaning, and I'm learning to set type."

"You must be smart."

"You could do it. How much do you make?"

"Thirty cents a day and board."

"Thirty cents a day! I make only thirty cents a week."

"Keelboat men make seventy-five cents a day plus board. But you should see the calluses on their shoulders! And you ought to see 'em fight."

"Why do they fight?"

"To see which crew is the best on the river."

"You live in St. Joe?"

"No, on a farm on the river, about six miles north."

"So do I, when I'm home," Neil said. "At Bend of the River."

"Hope we get a lot of rain so I can keep working the river. Else I'll have to go back and help farm. If dry weather sets and the river goes down we're out of luck."

"Do you want to be a farmer?"

"No!"

"Neither do I. I want to be a printer. Would your father mind if you didn't farm?"

"No. Would yours?"

"I think so." After a pause Neil said, "I got a sturgeon gristle the other day. First one I ever had."

"Me and my brother go spearing sturgeon at night."

"How do you see?"

"We put a platform on the boat and put a pile of mud on it and build a wood fire on it. I get on one end and he gets on the other. You have to hold the spear poles sideways to the current so your shadows won't be downstream. Then we can see 'em."

"How do you catch them?"

"Just hit 'em in the back of the head and stun 'em. Then drag 'em over the edge and kill 'em with an ax. Last one we got weighed 150 pounds."

"What do you do with them?"

"Sell 'em to old man Hess here for a dollar a piece. He smokes 'em and sells 'em in Chicago for smoked halibut."

The steamer bell began sounding, and Francis broke into a run. "Hey, I have to go—see you Saturday."

"I'll be here." Neil felt as though he'd talked to a world traveler. "I wonder if Clay knows about catching sturgeon at night? I'll ask him where he got that gristle."

The tenseness of the morning began to melt away by the time they cleared up to be ready for Uncle Bert. After reporting to Miss Van Vliet's landlady, they drove home to Aunt Annie's elegant supper. This meal was another step in her fight against slavery, and she had long wanted to meet Miss Van Vliet and give Mr. Rogers a change from Lutie's cooking.

"The trouble with Lutie Bibbins," Aunt Annie told Neil, "is that she has no imagination. She's the kind that would set a white hard-boiled egg on a white plate on a white tablecloth!"

Aunt Annie felt amply rewarded when Mr. Rogers

cut into a large piece of pie, its golden crust sparkling with sugar, and sighed, "It is downright sinful to enjoy food this much!"

As they cleared the dishes Miss Van Vliet told Aunt Annie, "It isn't possible for us to buy free-labor goods now. And the Quaker, Levi Coffin, is moving to Cincinnati next year so that he can operate a wholesale store for free-labor goods."

"Then we'll just have to bide our time," Aunt Annie said, "and see how his goods will be sent out."

Mr. Rogers shook his head, telling Uncle Bert about the council meeting. "Mrs. Waldie had to wait to complain about her broken window until the council threshed out whether the ordinance on cows should be worded 'cows running at large' or 'cows from committing trespass.'"

"I'll bet they chose 'cows from committing trespass.'"

"You're right, Bert. Most of the members have no use for abolitionists, so their sympathy was with the marshal when he said someone had broken into the pound and he couldn't watch windows and round up animals at the same time."

"I wonder if the person breaking into the pound could have been a good friend of the window breaker?" Uncle Bert asked.

Mr. Rogers looked at him with sudden understanding, his eyebrows up, his lips pursed.

Miss Van Vliet said she had received a letter from the Methodist church, disowning her. "I wasn't surprised. More and more people have been snubbing me each Sunday—they didn't approve of my writing about their problem with slavery."

Aunt Annie shook her head in disbelief. "You are welcome to come to church with us. Mr. Lord would be pleased. He told me how much he admired your courage in printing the paper."

Miss Van Vliet smiled and Aunt Annie noticed a sudden blush on her cheeks.

"Mr. Lord has trouble enough, Mrs. Jarvis. He doesn't need such a burden as I'd be."

Uncle Bert broke the silence that followed. "I think it would be a good thing if we forgot our troubles and played some euchre."

Mr. Rogers agreed. "We can beat these ladies any day, Bert."

Aunt Annie folded the cloth and Uncle Bert found the cards, counting out those needed for the game. Mr. Rogers shuffled and dealt, turning up a nine of spades. Neil, looking into Uncle Bert's hand, saw that with only two spades he was ordering Mr. Rogers to pick up that little spade.

"They'll go down, sure, if that's the only spade Mr. Rogers has," Neil thought. Yet the men squeezed through with three tricks, enough to win the hand.

"Well, Annie, you sent a boy to mill that time," Uncle Bert said as he trumped her trick. Aunt Annie played carefully, but time after time the men were lucky, taking just enough tricks to win the hand. Uncle Bert laughed and teased her, "We'll show you whose boar ate the cabbage!"

Soon Miss Van Vliet began to adopt his tactics and the contest became so close that Mr. Rogers kept repeating, "Now this is the crisis, partner. We must win this one."

Neil hated to have the evening end, but Aunt Annie said she wanted her guests home before dark settled in, so Uncle Bert went to hitch up Bessie.

As he helped put away the dishes, Neil asked, "Aunt Annie, do you think the men on the council know Mr. Rogers is an abolitionist?"

"They may suspect he is, and then they may think he's just a printer doing his job. He worked on the first newspaper in Niles for Miss Van Vliet's brother."

"I didn't know she had a brother."

"I think he went to Coldwater and started a paper there, but I heard he died. That's likely the reason she came back to Niles with his press. Be careful of that dish, Neil. That was a piece of my mother's silver-wedding china and I'm very choice of it."

Neil looked at the fat bowl with its pink flowers. "I think we have a dish like this at home, only the top got broken."

"Of course it did," Aunt Annie said crisply. "Your mother let the girls play with it."

Neil put the dish away in the cupboard in the buttery. He wondered, "Did it matter to Aunt Annie, even when they were young, that she wasn't slender and pretty like my mother?

"Grownups," he thought, "are hard to figure out. Uncle Bert, most of all. He's always calm, I never thought to see him so daring."

Neil leaned out the buttery window. "I wonder if I'd like being a printer for strangers, or if I only want to be a printer for Mr. Rogers and Miss Van Vliet? And how long can they go on with the paper now that people are beginning to cancel?"

He listened to the keening of a tree frog (Uncle Bert would say it was foretelling a coming rain). The eerie, lonely little frog cried trouble into Neil's heart. He knew Sam Gunn was winning.

8

The Beginning
of the End

The next weeks developed a rhythm of their own. Always, trouble appeared after the weekly Wednesday delivery. Neil found himself hoping, each week, that this time it might be different—that the trouble would just go away.

Tuesday morning, as they carried in wood, Neil asked Clay, "Has anyone seen Sam Gunn lately?"

Clay was emphatic. "You don't have to see him. He's here. Sam Gunn won't ever go away. Not his men, either, not till he gets what he's after."

"He's after slaves, isn't he?"

Clay nodded.

"I wish he'd go look for them in some other place and leave us be."

"Sam Gunn's not goin' to look any place else, Neil." After a pause Clay added, "'Cause we got us a river."

Neil was puzzled. He put his armful of wood down and stood, looking at Clay.

"Easier movin' on a river." Clay put his finger to his lips.

Still puzzled, thinking hard, Neil continued to look at Clay.

The following day Neil stopped to deliver Ancel's

paper and said, "I might as well take time to get this pesky tongue sewn, Mr. Hawkins, else I'll have to stop and pull it back all morning."

Ancel did the repair himself. "I see Mr. Rogers got your window fixed. Sure hope you don't have any more trouble. There, that'll hold."

Neil laced his shoe. "I hope not. How much do I owe you, sir?"

"You don't owe me anything, Cornelius." Ancel leaned on the counter. "Seems to me you're getting back from your delivering earlier than you used to."

"It's a lot easier going now, although the mud gets awful bad sometimes. Thanks, Mr. Hawkins, I intended to pay."

As he went up the hill Neil determined to come in at the back door. "No need to advertise we don't have much business."

He was not long into the day before he found that Clay was right; Sam Gunn hadn't gone away. Proof lay in a note that Mr. LaPierre slipped to him, urging him to take it to Miss Van Vliet immediately, with no further stops along the way.

Miss Van Vliet took the note to the pressroom to read to Mr. Rogers. She was so astonished she had to sit down.

"Sam Gunn's man offered Mr. Alexander a thousand dollars to reveal the hiding places for the slaves here!"

"What did Alexander say?" Mr. Rogers asked.

She read, "You've watched my house and you've watched my stable—you know I've not moved from either place. You ought to be satisfied soon that I'm not your man!"

Mr. Rogers looked at Neil. "We trust you, Neil, letting you hear this. We trust, also, that you will forget hearing anything about hiding places for slaves."

"Yes, sir."

Snatches of thought tumbled about in Neil's head as he walked home. "More is going on than I know, and I wish I knew more!"

After supper Uncle Bert read the petition aloud.

Forms of Petition:

To the Honorable, the Senate and House of Representatives of the State of Michigan:

The petition of the undersigned citizens of the County of _____ respectfully shows that your petitioners are opposed to the annexation of new slave territory to the U.S. and to the increase of slavery.

They therefore pray your Honorable body to pass a resolution, addressed to the Congress of the U.S. declaring that no project for the annexation of Texas to the U.S. or its territory should be entertained by the Government until slavery shall be wholly and forever abolished within the limits of the former.

The chains of poor slaves are clanking, as it were, in the ears and what we do in behalf of these unfortunate fellow beings should be speedily done. Circulate the petition.

Aunt Annie put down her mending and with her scissors clipped the petition from the paper. "Bring the pen and ink, please, Neil. Now, Bert, here is our chance to do something." Both of them signed the petition and Aunt Annie addressed an envelope.

Uncle Bert continued reading. "Here is something! Miss Van Vliet is defending herself against the Methodists."

> To steal a neighbor's horse is an evil to society and is therefore legislated upon politically. It is also a violation of good morals, and therefore horse thieves are excluded from the Church. Yet when a man is stolen from Africa the slaveowner is allowed to sit in Church and the woman who speaks out against his moral evil is excluded from Church. Perhaps the Church should write a Southern Bible?

"Good for her," Aunt Annie said. "In too many churches, seems to me, the shepherds are being driven by the sheep."

"Here is your Shakespeare quotation, Annie.

> Rough winds do shake the darling buds of May,
> And summer's lease hath all too short a date."

Aunt Annie smiled.

"Here's an item saying brigs of six hundred and four hundred slaves are arriving in Brazil."

Aunt Annie stopped smiling.

"Here's another: 'The slave schooner *Rio de Janeiro* has been taken with 400 captives on the African coast by the British cruiser *Ferret.*'"

Neil asked, "Why are you smiling now, Aunt Annie?"

"Because England frees all slaves," she said.

Uncle Bert continued, "Miss Van Vliet has two ads out of Southern papers for runaway slaves:

The subscriber's servant has run away. He had one ear cropped off and his back was badly cut up. . . .

$50 reward. Ran away from subscriber, his Negro man Paul. I understand Gen. R. Y. Hayne has purchased his wife and children and has them on his estate where, no doubt, the fellow is frequently lurking.

"That ought to bring home a few facts of life to people whose families aren't being broken up," Aunt Annie said.

"If anybody is reading," Neil worried. "We've had so many cancellations."

Uncle Bert thought a moment. "Neil, I think you should tell Miss Van Vliet that you don't feel you should accept pay any more. Everyone has to do some good in this world, and you'll be doing your bit when you deliver for her."

Aunt Annie agreed. "You tell her you talked it over with us, and we approve. After all, you have a place to sleep, and food to eat, and clothes to wear. Not as though you were an orphan. And you'll be going back home any day now."

Neil heard the last sentence in shock. He could scarcely wait to get to the comfortable darkness of his room. "Go home again—of course I want to see them all, and Shep—but leave Miss Van Vliet and Mr. Rogers and the wonderful talk? Now that they're in trouble?"

He could not get to sleep. How, he worried, would he ever get back to working on a paper if he left the *Star of Freedom?* How could he explain to his folks that he wanted to know what was happening in the whole country, not just at Bend of the River? Now he was letting his thoughts hurry and Mr. Rogers said he must not. . . . He pulled the blanket over his head in an effort to stop them.

Neil felt he had just fallen asleep when a woodpecker began drumming him out of bed. He stepped down onto the rug precisely, lest any sudden movement cause his world to spill. He made his bed, smoothing each wrinkle, tucking each corner, willing the world to perfection.

He chewed his breakfast carefully, quietly, and cleared away his dishes. Before he left for work he filled the woodbox and took the slops to the pigs. He helped to pack his dinner box and Aunt Annie watched him walk down the road and wondered aloud, "Is that boy sick?"

On his way to work Neil closed his eyes whenever he heard a bird call, concentrating, trying to identify fifty different calls; trying to keep his mind on something besides trouble.

With his eyes closed, Neil smelled the green world. He could tell that he was nearing Mr. Showdy's blacksmith shop when he smelled the manure at the end of the lane. The sharp, bitter odor of the tannery wafted up from the river, and the rich smells of the spices and coffee beans and smoked fish came from the storehouses. Last of all, the enticing smell of fresh-baked bread from Mr. Pennell's bakery let him know he was close to the barbershop and Main Street. Already long lines of wagons were waiting to unload at the wharves.

"Everywhere there is bustle," Neil thought, "everywhere, except at the *Star of Freedom.*"

The moment he opened the door, Neil said, "I don't want you to pay me, ma'am. Aunt Annie and Uncle Bert think the same."

Miss Van Vliet, smiling, turned at her desk. "Thank you, Neil. Come out to the pressroom."

She told Mr. Rogers what Neil proposed. "I think that we will have to stop publication soon. We won't say anything to anyone—just keep on until our supply of paper is gone. But I can't order more."

The bell jingled as the door opened. Mr. Rogers and Neil listened to a man tell Miss Van Vliet, "I would like to caution the public!"

"About what, sir?"

"About William Wilber the watch repairer. I paid him seventy-five cents with the understanding that he would bring my silver watch to me."

"Hasn't he done this?" Miss Van Vliet asked.

"I have demanded the watch several times and he refuses to produce it. He is totally irresponsible."

"Could you not sue him to recover the watch?"

"I cannot afford to pay the costs to pursue a course of law to reclaim it, but I at least intend to caution the public about doing business with him."

"Our circulation is not large, sir. Perhaps you would rather insert this notice in Mr. Cook's paper, the *Republican*."

"I have already placed it there. I want to warn everyone not to patronize this watch man!"

"Very well, sir." Miss Van Vliet bent her head and wrote the copy.

The bell jingled again as the man left and Mr. Rogers grinned, shaking his head at Neil.

107

"What will you do, Mr. Rogers, when the paper stops?"

"I might see if anyone needs a printer in Berrien."

Disconsolately, Neil took the bag from the hook next to the fire bucket and went for the mail. At the post office he saw Tom Huston.

"You carrying the mail again, Tom?"

Tom nodded. "Until the rains stop, and the stage can get through. I brought a letter to your paper gal from Berrien."

"You walked from Berrien this morning?"

"My brother let me use his horse because I have to take mail on to St. Joe when I get back."

Neil envied Tom his important job. Tom was only thirteen, and when he got the job he had to take an oath on the Bible never to open any mail and read it.

Picking up his papers and stuffing them into his bag, Neil hurried out, anxious to tell Miss Van Vliet there was a letter to be paid for. Suddenly he was jolted by a tremendous shove and then tripped, his feet flying out from under him, the papers scattering from the mailbag into the mud. It happened so fast; he was concerned only with quickly picking up each piece, losing nothing to the wind.

Slowly he walked the short distance back to the office. He opened the door carefully and closed it quietly. All his care had not, after all, kept the morning from spilling over.

"I'm sorry about the mail, Miss Van Vliet. I think I can wipe the mud off."

"How did it happen, Neil?"

"I forgot to watch out for Fats."

9

There Are More Things in Heaven and Earth . . .

If Neil needed any further proof that Sam Gunn had not left Niles, or that he was reading the paper and being angered by it, that proof was painfully evident the following morning. Ten panes of glass had been broken out of the *Freedom's* windows—five on each side of the door!

Miss Van Vliet entered the office and saw Neil looking in, through the jagged glass, from the outside. She never spoke. She skirted the glass, her mouth set in anger, and went straight to her desk.

It remained for Mr. Rogers, coming in from the pressroom, to unlock the front door and admit Neil. He had never known such a grim, quiet morning; he had never seen so much broken glass. He spent the morning sweeping and wiping it up.

As he swept, Neil found himself remembering Sam Gunn as he had seen him that day at the hotel. There was a stillness about him that reminded Neil of the western rattlesnake he and Clay had seen at the circus. The rattler had been just that still. Even their eyes were alike—hard, unblinking, and cold.

Miss Van Vliet wrote for the coming edition:

This Village No Longer Law-Abiding

Is someone bribing the Marshall to look the other way as windows in our village continue to be broken? Sam Gunn is still in our midst. Niles must recall how he enticed the cook from the steamer *Algoma*. Will you let him steal another man?

CAUTION!!

Colored People of Niles, one and all, you are hereby respectfully cautioned and advised to avoid conversing with strangers and Slave Stealers! Therefore if you value your LIBERTY and the welfare of the Fugitives among you SHUN them in every possible manner, as so many HOUNDS on the track of the most unfortunate of your race.

When Neil saw these editorials set in type he thought, "Sam Gunn will read them; for the first time he'll see his name in print. How and where and when will he strike then? Miss Van Vliet will never be safe again!"

Mr. Rogers was just as concerned. He and Neil looked at one another a long time, knowing argument was useless.

"Aunt Annie," Neil thought, "would be writing the same editorials if her windows were twice broken, and hers aren't half as big as these."

By tacit agreement Neil and Mr. Rogers tried to protect Miss Van Vliet. Mr. Rogers stopped by for her each morning and walked her home after work.

All week the fear sat in Neil's stomach. He ate, scarcely knowing what he had swallowed. He did not tell Aunt Annie and Uncle Bert about the coming editorials. "I don't think that Sam Gunn will do anything till after the paper comes out next Wednesday. If Wednesday ever comes, the way time's going."

Miss Van Vliet said, the following week, "Few in Niles will read the paper this week, but a great many around the country will read it."

She was wrong—every copy sold. The word spread and men stopped to buy and see for themselves just what kind of woman thought, first, that she could go into business printing a paper, and, second, have the courage to fight Sam Gunn!

It also turned out to be a day of sun and wind and high white clouds chasing across a blue sky. As always Neil looked forward to his last delivery, on the west side of the river.

Miss Sarah and Miss Lina came out to the porch, pleased to see him. "Good afternoon, Cornelius."

"Why is the coop up here by the porch, Miss Sarah?"

"We have moved Emmaline's home because she has new babies and can't leave them."

Neil watched Emmaline crawling into the hole of the coop. "When did she have them?"

"After thy visit last week we noticed she was pushing all the hay outside and we knew she would have them."

"We think there are five," Miss Lina said.

"Why did she push the hay out?"

"She didn't want the babies to get tangled in it and suffocate; they're only two inches long. The next night she put all the hay back."

Neil refused refreshment, for he had no wish to be present when Miss Sarah and Miss Lina read the editorials. "They are so gentle. They will be shocked and worried."

He returned to the office and found the window glass replaced.

Miss Van Vliet explained, "Mr. Hawkins came and helped, but Mr. Rogers cut his hand. We couldn't stop the bleeding so he's gone to Dr. Finley's for a stitch, likely. He'll be back soon."

"I feel as if I should stay all night and protect the windows, Miss Van Vliet, but I'll see you in the morning."

Clay was waiting at his back door. "I was going to help Mr. Rogers, but I saw Ancel Hawkins there. So I figured to stay home."

"Does your pa know what Miss Van Vliet wrote?"

Clay nodded. "He's worried."

"So am I."

The boys looked at one another, shaking their heads.

"You watch for Mr. Rogers to come back, Clay, because Miss Van Vliet is there alone."

Clay nodded. "I'll stay here."

"Oh!" Neil snapped his fingers. "I've left my jacket. I'll have to get it. I'm coming to work real early in the morning and it'll be cold."

Neil started toward the office, then turned. "Hey, Clay, I almost forgot to tell you—Emmaline has five babies!"

The shades were pulled so Neil went around to the back, coming with practiced step through the dark

112

storeroom and pressroom. When he opened the office door Miss Van Vliet was standing before her desk, one hand on the top. Neil was astonished. The entire central section of the desk seemed to have been lifted—her hand seemed to be pulling it up.

"Oh!" She drew in her breath sharply, turning to stand before the desk.

"I didn't mean to scare you, Miss Van Vliet. I left my jacket. What happened to the desk?"

For a long moment Miss Van Vliet looked at Neil. Shaking her head slightly, she said, "Oh, Neil, it would be better if I didn't tell you. I've no right to burden you."

"Burden me with what, Miss Van Vliet?"

"I know I can trust you, Neil, but I truly have no right. . . ."

"Yes, you can, Miss Van Vliet." Neil waited.

"I'm so troubled, Neil. In the event that something should happen that I won't be here. . . ."

"When, Miss Van Vliet? Why won't you be here?"

"In case of an accident, or if I should be called away. . . ." Finally she sighed. "I'll show you something about this desk."

Carefully, she moved the central section down; it swung easily and fitted smoothly, just as Neil had always seen it.

"There is a way for you to lift this, Neil. Come and open this little center door. Can you feel a slight depression behind it?"

Neil nodded as his finger explored and found the depression.

"Now press and push toward the left."

A small piece of wood slid when Neil pushed. Miss Van Vliet lifted carefully and the entire central section swung up. Behind it were document boxes concealed by the flanking pilasters. At the bottom of the series of pigeonholes was another small flat secret drawer.

"In case I would not be here I want you to look in this little drawer, if you are alone. Only if you are alone. If there is a note, get it to Dr. Finley. Could you do that?"

Neil nodded.

"Now I want you to try to get into the desk this time by yourself."

Neil had no trouble; he was filled with admiration for the cabinetmaker who had created such a marvel.

"I may be punished for telling you this, Neil, but sometimes things happen so fast and I may as well tell you another secret. If you would need to help Brother Levi load this clock, you must know something about it. You must be able to show him."

Miss Van Vliet took Neil's arm and moved with him to the end of the room where the tall case clock stood. She opened the door and pointed to two knotholes in the panel behind the wooden works. In the lower one she put her finger, giving a twist.

"When you have it crosswise, Neil, push right. It moves easily." Then she slid the panel back. "There is room for a man to stand in the back, behind this panel. You must lift your feet to step over and duck your head, holding the works to one side." She closed the panel. "Now I want you to try."

"I turn it crosswise and then move it right, just the

114

opposite of the desk?" Neil wondered if the same cabinetmaker had made this clock.

"Yes. If you were inside, Neil, and wanted out, you would turn the knothole the opposite way. The knotholes in the back can be moved for breathing. Neil, please promise me you won't tell anyone any of this? Not even Mr. Rogers? He has enough to worry about."

"I won't tell anyone, Miss Van Vliet."

"I know it isn't right for me to tell you, and I know your Uncle Bert would be angry if he knew. But I do feel so relieved, Neil, now that I've done it."

Neil slid the panel back and closed the clock door without disturbing the pendulum, still ticking away. They both glanced at the desk to be sure the top had been replaced. Then they went out the back door where the fragrance of honeysuckle was drifting up from the riverbank.

Miss Van Vliet locked the door behind them and Neil walked with her up Cedar Street hill to her rooming house. At the steps she turned and said, "Maybe things will all work out by the week's end, Neil. If you meet Mr. Rogers, will you tell him you've seen me home?"

Neil ran a lot of the way home, his thoughts running with him. "What does Brother Levi intend to do with the clock in Virginia? Is he going to bring a slave back in it? Was Miss Van Vliet going to put a note in the desk when I came in? Or was she looking for one? Who would have put it there? What did she mean when she said something might happen that she wouldn't be here? She wouldn't leave unless someone made her leave. She said in case of an accident . . . if Sam Gunn did something to her, it wouldn't be an accident . . . I'm scared. I'm scared for her."

10

Foul Deeds Will Rise

The first bird sang at four o'clock. Neil heard it. He thought of Miss Van Vliet. He thought of Sam Gunn. He lay quietly, hearing more bird song. Then, very early, he heard Uncle Bert go to the kitchen and stoke the fire in the stove.

Neil jumped out of bed, anxious to move the day forward, anxious to get to work extra early, since that was the only way he could think of to protect Miss Van Vliet. He hurried through breakfast and chores, as spendthrift with time as he had been cautious of it yesterday.

Aunt Annie was up extra early, also. Since reading the editorials she and Uncle Bert were very worried.

"Neil," Uncle Bert said, "I'm coming for you tonight. I don't want you walking home."

Aunt Annie warned, "Be careful, Neil. Your folks would never forgive us if anything happened to you."

"Nothing is going to happen to me, Aunt Annie. I won't be out delivering today." He didn't add that there would not even be another edition in preparation, since he had promised Miss Van Vliet that he would say nothing about that.

Counting as he went, Neil walked fifty steps and

then ran fifty steps all the way to work, down Sycamore Street hill and over to Main Street. The shades were still drawn on most of the shop windows as well as on the *Freedom's* windows, and no windows were broken!

Neil tried the front door. Finding it locked, he slipped between the buildings and ran around to the back. The door wasn't barred.

Neil opened the door to the pressroom and stood, aghast. Utter devastation met his eyes! The great press was tipped over and smashed; the devil's tail lay to one side, broken off. All the type was thrown from the cases. The light from the window fell on papers, scattered, and on spilled ink.

Fearfully, Neil entered the office. Every drawer in the desk had been emptied and the contents thrown about. The stacks of paper beneath the counter were pulled out and underfoot. Open-mouthed, numb, Neil stared until he became aware of heavy steps, and voices, and the back door opening. Strange voices, coming closer.

Neil took a quick step toward the front door before he remembered it was locked! He whirled about toward the clock. He opened the outer door, felt for the knothole, and twisted it crosswise and right. The panel slid back. He ducked his head and stepped inside the first space, turning into the back, pulling the clock door shut, giving the pendulum a slight push before sliding the panel back at the moment the men entered the office.

He held his breath, his heart pounding, his mouth feeling as if it were filled with cotton. He listened.

"Doesn't look as if she'll be printing any more editorials here. I know she brought a slave in from South Bend sometime in the night. Where's she got him? My men didn't find a clue here."

The sound of a fist slapping a palm came to Neil. "How's she doing it? In the last two weeks we've followed all of 'em, especially Doc Finley. The only other go-between we can see is the kid, delivering, and we've never seen them give him anything. They haven't even talked to each other in the past two weeks, but they're all in it together. She's directing LaPierre and Alexander and Comley at the mill—he's LaPierre's son-in-law! Nigger Bill's in it, too! Someone is signaling her that they've got a slave holed up. But no one has come near her. They've got to be doing it in writing!"

Neil was certain he was listening to Sam Gunn. The voice wasn't loud, but it was curt and hard. "They've managed to move slaves on this route for the last four months. They've got this one holed up on the river somewhere. We've got him pinned down to a mile. I know he's hurt bad and he's not going to be easy to move. We've got every road covered so they're going to have to move him on the river and we've covered that to below the mill. I've put men on the islands and the bridge. We're following everyone today and, by the gods, we'll get him. We'll get him tonight!"

There was a pause. Then, with a dreadful finality that brought a tingling up the back of Neil's neck, Sam Gunn said, "If we don't, she'll tell us where she's got him. She'll tell."

Slow steps came toward the clock. The clock door opened. Someone looked in. Neil held his hand over

119

his heart, lest it be heard. Through the knothole, he caught a whiff of sweet licorice. It seemed a long time before the clock door swung shut. Neil swallowed. The steps moved from the office, through the pressroom. He judged there were three men. Straining, Neil thought he heard the back door close.

He forced himself to remain in the clock for a much longer time than he wished, fearful that the man who had looked inside might have remained, watching. He began to sweat. He was thankful there was no key in the clock door. The stranger might have turned it, locking him in. "This clock could have been my coffin!" He was thankful he had not sneezed. He was thankful that he had started the pendulum going again. He thought he heard a kitten mewing and then realized he was imagining.

He thought about all he had heard. Sam Gunn said they were all in this together—even Clay's father. Clay was right about the river! "Oh, dear God," he prayed, "don't let them hurt Miss Van Vliet. Where is she? What will they do to her to make her tell? I have to get out of here and look in the desk!"

Carefully Neil slid the panel back. Holding the works, he opened the outer door of the clock, a quarter-inch at a time. He saw no one. He stepped out, sliding the panel back, starting the pendulum swinging again before he closed the outer door.

He tiptoed to the door and peered into the pressroom. It was empty. He moved quickly back to the desk, opening the center door. His finger in the depression, he moved it left until the small piece of wood moved. Holding his breath, he carefully lifted the desk

120

top. He opened the little drawer and found a note! He shoved it into his pocket and lifted the desk top down.

From the pressroom, he looked out into the storeroom. When his eyes adjusted to the dark, and he was certain the room was empty, he went out as quickly and as silently as possible.

"How will I get this note to Dr. Finley, now that they're watching so close? I could go to Mr. Rogers at his rooming house, but I promised Miss Van Vliet not to bother him."

Neil decided that he would ask Ancel's help. Ancel had been good to him, tipping a penny each week, sewing the tongue in his shoe, and helping Mr. Rogers with the windows. He walked around to the front of the shoe shop. The men were just coming to work, just pulling up the shades. Neil went in and Ancel came to the counter.

"Morning, Cornelius. You're up early."

"Yes, Mr. Haw . . . kins." Neil caught his breath. From Ancel came the same sweet scent of licorice that he had caught through the knothole! Something in Neil's chest wanted to burst, but he shrugged and asked, "Have you seen Mr. Rogers? He said he was coming in early, but the door's locked."

"No, I haven't seen him. Wonder how his hand is?"

"I don't know. Miss Van Vliet said he cut it. Well, I guess I could go watch Mr. Showdy shoe horses awhile."

Neil sauntered across the street, stopping to talk to Judge Brown. Out of the corner of his eye he could see

Ancel standing in the door, watching. Neil forced himself to go slowly to the blacksmith shop.

Normally he would enjoy watching Mr. Showdy fan the charcoal with his huge bellows, but this morning he was glad that the men were busy getting an ox into the sling for shoeing. No one noticed that he entered on Main and left by the side door on Second Street. He glanced toward Main Street and there stood Ancel, his back to Showdy's—detained, having to talk to another man!

Neil took a giant step into the alley and ran as fast as he could down to Front Street. Clay stepped out of the lane.

"Where you going?"

"They wrecked the place. I don't know where Miss Van Vliet is, or Mr. Rogers."

"Where you going?"

"To Mr. Lord." Neil ran to the corner, looking up Main Street. When he saw no sign of Ancel he dashed quickly across the street and started up an alley. At Third Street Neil cut over and started up the steep alley that would bring him close to the parsonage. Looking up, he saw Fats standing at the top of the hill blocking his way.

"You're in a mighty hurry, ain't you?"

All Neil's pent-up anxiety burst out in blazing anger. He never stopped running. He stooped down and scooped up some rocks.

"Get out of my way!" Neil let go with a rock that he gauged would just barely miss Fats's head.

Fats put his hands up to his head and Neil sent a handful of rocks toward Fats's legs.

122

"I can't hurt his middle, but if I can hit his legs he'll put his hands down and I'll get his wrists."

Getting closer, his aim even better, Neil kept scooping up rocks, throwing as fast as he could. "Get out of my way, you dirty slob!"

"Ouch!" One rock hit Fats's leg, another his hand.

"The next one's coming through your skull!"

Neil was nearing the hilltop, still holding a handful of rocks, and determined to use every one. He threw another, hard. It must have hurt, for Fats turned with a yell and ran down Third Street. Neil threw his last rock and caught Fats right in the middle of the back.

Neil leaned against the corner of a building, catching his breath. Fats was out of sight, but Neil was still worried about Ancel and decided against approaching the parsonage from Fourth Street. He ran down Fifth Street and cut into the back yard of the parsonage, knocking rapidly on the kitchen door.

"Please, could I come in and see Mr. Lord?" he asked as soon as the housekeeper appeared.

"He's eating breakfast. Can't you come back later?"

"No, ma'am!"

Perhaps Neil sounded desperate, for Mr. Lord came out to the kitchen. "What's the matter, Neil? Something wrong?"

"Could we go in your office, sir?"

"Right through here."

When Mr. Lord closed the door, Neil said, "I've got to get a note to Dr. Finley, but I can't take it. They're watching."

"Who is?"

"Sam Gunn's men."

"Do you have the note?"

Neil took it from his pocket and Mr. Lord read it aloud, puzzled. "Out of this nettle, danger, we pluck this flower, safety."

"Miss Van Vliet told me to take it to Dr. Finley, sir. I wasn't to tell anyone, not even Mr. Rogers. I nearly told Ancel Hawkins, but just as I started to ask him to help I smelled licorice."

"You what?"

"The same smell I smelled in the clock."

"Could you begin at the beginning, Neil?"

Neil did. When he had finished, Mr. Lord asked, concerned, "You didn't see Mr. Rogers or Miss Van Vliet at all this morning?"

Neil shook his head, swallowing hard.

"You did exactly right to come to me; I can go to Dr. Finley without being suspected. Now I want you to wait here until I return. Do not leave, Neil, under any circumstances. I'll come straight back."

From the door, Neil watched Mr. Lord saddle his black mare in a moment's time and then continue down the street, sedately, carrying his Bible. His housekeeper brought a plate of cookies and a mug of hot cocoa for Neil and sat with him.

"I hope those ladies down the street noticed how nice and slow Mr. Lord is stepping out. They've been doing a lot of talking about him being a lover of fast horses. He has to go all over for the church, and he needs a good horse. I always tell him to ride slow around the village and when he goes to Edwardsburg to preach then's the time he can ride fast."

Neil was glad for the housekeeper's kindly chatter, but the hot cocoa melted none of his chill fear.

11

Steps on the Stairs

Neil was waiting at the back door when Mr. Lord returned. "Does Dr. Finley know where they are?"

"Not yet. He wants to talk to you, but he doesn't want to come here since they've seen me visiting him once today."

"What should I do?"

"He suggested you go fishing along the river until you think you are near Miss Sarah's. Go up through the woods to her place and wait for him."

"Where will I get a pole?"

"I have one in the barn, and I'll dig some worms."

Neil remembered, when he was in the clock, that the voice had said there were men on the islands and on the bridge. "Maybe," he thought, "they won't be there; it's not noon yet."

He was wrong. A man was lounging on the west side of the bridge and a boy was fishing from the middle. Neil thought it wise to stop and talk to the boy, who was fishing with a snare.

"Having any luck?"

"Not yet."

"How do you know when to jerk the wire?"

"You watch the fish and when you see one run its head in the noose you jerk when you think the loop is behind the gills."

Neil stayed another five minutes and then sauntered across, past the man, looking at the water. His mouth felt dry and his stomach bottomless.

At the end of the bridge Neil climbed down the bank, walking along the shore, watching the quiet water. He was careful to put out his line and sit on the bank within sight of the man on the bridge. He hoped he might catch a fish for Miss Sarah and Miss Lina. After a time he felt a tug and thought he had only to haul the line in, but the fish was very scrappy. It was some time before he was able to bring in a bass that he judged would weigh close to two pounds.

He abandoned fishing, willing himself to move along slowly. He saw no one. Sometimes he stopped to count turtles in case he was being watched. Always he counted the rowboats along the river and remembered their location.

Past the islands, he struck out through the brush and up the bank. The land leveled out for a time and then began another steep slope. On this second stage of the hill, just below Miss Sarah's, Neil came upon a small cabin. He was startled to see it there, hidden among the trees. As he approached the big house, he noticed Emmaline near the porch and thought it would be wise to call.

Miss Lina came to the side door and escorted him past Emmaline's watchful eye.

"I thought you and Miss Sarah might like a fish for supper."

"And what a fine fish! Thee are most thoughtful, Cornelius."

Both ladies turned to him. "Thee are not working today?"

"We're all caught up this afternoon, Miss Lina."

Miss Lina and Miss Sarah folded their hands and looked at one another.

Miss Sarah said, "Sit down, Cornelius, and tell us all."

"I'm supposed to meet Dr. Finley."

Miss Sarah and Miss Lina looked at one another again.

"Why is Dr. Finley going to meet thee here?"

"I'm not supposed to tell, Miss Lina."

"Would it ease thee in thy mind," Miss Sarah asked, "if we were to tell thee that when Dr. Finley comes he will have thee tell all?"

Neil never had to make that decision, for Dr. Finley came then, his horse cantering up the drive. He brought his bag and put it on the table.

"They're following me. I must pretend I'm on a call. Mr. Rogers has been hurt, Neil. Lutie said he had an early breakfast because he wanted to get to work extra early. It was dark when he left the house. She was in the kitchen and heard nothing. Some time later she heard a call and found him with a bad blow at the back of his head."

"Is he all right?"

"I hope so, given time. Lutie feels it was a robbery because his pockets had been turned out. I think Gunn's men were looking for this note that you found."

Dr. Finley put the note on the table and for the first

time Neil noticed that it was a newspaper clipping that had been pasted to notepaper. He also noticed that neither Miss Lina nor Miss Sarah seemed interested in it.

"Did you go to Miss Van Vliet's?"

"Her landlady said the same—that she'd gone to work extra early." Dr. Finley looked worried. "Now I want your story, Neil."

Neil tried to recall everything he had heard. When he finished, Dr. Finley said, "You've done a fine, fine job. I want you to stay here. We may need you tonight."

"Could you tell Aunt Annie and Uncle Bert, sir? They're worried."

"Mr. Lord has already told them, Neil." Dr. Finley looked out at the men on horseback patroling the road. "For once I'm glad they've followed me; it will fit right in with Mr. Lord's plan."

Miss Sarah went with the doctor to the porch, where he opened his case in view of the men. He poured powder into a paper and twisted the ends, talking to her all the while. Then he tipped his hat and left. At a discreet distance, the men followed.

Neil went to the door to watch Emmaline tend her babies. Miss Sarah came and stood with him.

"Sometimes waiting is the hardest thing in life, Cornelius."

Neil thought he might be sick. Miss Van Vliet could be hit on the head and lying bleeding like Mr. Rogers. . . . And Ancel. . . .

"How can it happen, Miss Sarah that someone you think is good turns out to be bad?"

"Count thyself fortunate, Cornelius, to find out early; thee will then be aware all thy life that people, for many reasons, may prove false."

Miss Van Vliet and Mr. Rogers hadn't been fooled by Ancel the way he had . . . was Sam Gunn paying him for spying? . . . Clay was right about Ancel at the tannery. . . . Neil's thoughts went in circles.

Miss Lina brought molasses cookies and a pot of hot tea to the table. "There is no trouble in life, Cornelius, that will not be helped by a good cup of tea."

Miss Sarah and Miss Lina sat at the kitchen table with Neil, their quiet speech dropping into the late afternoon as gently as drifting feathers. Holding the hot cup, sipping the strong tea softened with cream, Neil's stomach began to settle.

"Thee must be a most trustworthy young man or Miss Van Vliet would not have told thee about the drawer in the desk, or about the clock."

"I came back, Miss Lina, and saw it open. She had to tell."

"No. She trusted thee. We all do."

After a silence Miss Sarah said, "A great task faces us tonight. We will need thy help. We ask that thee not reveal to thy family or friends anything that happens."

Neil nodded, puzzled.

They looked at him a long while. Miss Lina added, "Lives depend on such secrecy."

Neil nodded again, though he was unsure what was to be secret.

"Dr. Finley will try tonight to move the slave here."

"Where will Dr. Finley find the slave, Miss Sarah?"

"Dr. Finley's instructions are contained in the note thee found." To Neil's astonishment, she quoted, " 'Out of this nettle, danger, we pluck this flower, safety.' Dr. Finley will go to the place of the nettles."

Miss Lina told him, "The Indians call it the Place of the Great Nettles."

"The slave is going to be hiding in nettles?" Neil's face showed his doubt.

"Precisely. That is why the hiding place has been successful. No one wishes to enter there." Miss Lina reached across the table and held Neil's hand. "Within the nettles there is a small underground room. It is this secret, more than any other, that we ask thee to guard."

Miss Sarah spoke. "If thee betray us, Cornelius, it is likely no slave will be able to escape again by this method, on this river. If thee betray us, even by so much as a glance, or a syllable, thee may have cost a man his life."

Neil's eyes promised for him. "I won't ever tell, ma'am."

"Thee must not tell a soul, not thy parents, not thy friends, never in thy lifetime. We would not take thee into our confidence, Cornelius, except that it may be necessary for thee to know before this night is over."

Neil nodded. "Did the quotations that Miss Van Vliet put in the paper show where to look for slaves?"

"Sometimes."

"When I was in the clock, Sam Gunn said Miss Van Vliet was directing everybody. He didn't say anything about Brother Levi or you."

130

"We trust Mr. Gunn has never heard of us."

Miss Sarah looked at Miss Lina, who seemed to nod slightly. "I will tell thee that one day when we lived in Ohio a slave came to our house from across the river. He was quaking in fear. He was encased in neck irons with prongs that extended up and over his head."

Miss Lina said, "That iron entered our souls."

Miss Sarah continued, "To help him meant that we must break the laws of the land, but they are manmade laws. We chose to obey the divine law. Our consciences bade us seek a blacksmith and a doctor and ever since we have been helping."

Miss Lina went to get some seeds and garbage to give Emmaline and Ebenezer. "It is best, Cornelius, that thee stay in the house while we feed the horses."

Neil sat, thinking about the doctor who helped the slave in Ohio. Uncle Bert said Dr. Finley had moved to Niles from Ohio . . . and the Quaker lady who had given Miss Van Vliet the medal . . . Miss Sarah and Miss Lina were Quakers . . . had they all known one another, earlier . . . who had clipped the quotation? . . . from what newspaper? . . . mysteries, all . . . he had a hunch that they might remain so . . . that he should ask no questions. . . .

Dusk came stealthily. The women fixed a light supper, knowing that for them the day was only beginning. Before they could sit at table, Mr. Lord and Dr. Finley called softly. Miss Lina went to pet Emmaline.

Neil hurried to the door. "Did you find Miss Van Vliet?"

Dr. Finley put his arm about Neil. "Not yet, but others are searching."

Neil's fist tightened. "What did Aunt Annie and Uncle Bert say?"

"They're ready to help," Mr. Lord said.

"How did thee cross the river?" Miss Lina asked.

"A sympathetic parishioner who doesn't want anyone to know he is sympathetic brought us across in his boat. He has fishing gear in case he's stopped."

In this forested place the darkness was falling fast. They sat down and Miss Sarah asked that their prayers be silent. In that moment they heard heavy footsteps coming slowly up the stairs. Mr. Lord and Neil looked up, startled.

Neil's heart pounded as he listened to the inexorable march up those steps. He managed to swallow. Then he screamed. The scream had almost to fight its way out in a kind of despairing gurgle.

"What's the matter, Neil?" Dr. Finley came quickly to his side.

His eyes wide, as the cellar door opened, Neil finally cried out, "I know where Miss Van Vliet is!"

Danger!

The room exploded in talk. Everyone talked, except Neil. He sat spellbound as the cellar door slowly opened, admitting Mr. Jason the mushroom man!

Mr. Lord and Dr. Finley asked together, "Where is she?"

"In the cellar at the office."

"The cellar!"

Neil explained, "I thought this morning that I heard the steps and the voices and the door opening all at once. Now I know I heard the steps first, and that they were coming up from the cellar. Then I heard the voices. Then I heard the door opening. When I stayed in the clock I thought I heard a kitten mewing. It must have been Miss Van Vliet. We don't have a cat at the *Star of Freedom.*"

"Where is the cellar door?" Mr. Lord was getting into his jacket.

"Inside the back door. To the right. It's a small trap door. We never use it. You can't see it because of all the barrels and boxes piled on it."

Dr. Finley caught Mr. Lord by the arm. "You must not go down alone. Get someone to help. If you don't you may be hit over the head. You'll have been no help at all."

"I promise."

Miss Sarah went with him to the barn to saddle her horse. "There will be someone on the bridge, Mr. Lord. Thee would be wise to go slowly."

Neil's eyes must have expressed his longing to go, for Dr. Finley put an arm about his shoulders.

"I need help tonight, Neil, and it seems you're elected."

Suddenly Neil felt as strong as one of the keelmen on the river, ready to help as well as Mr. Lord would have.

Dr. Finley asked, "You think it's dark enough, Mr. Jason?"

"Won't get any darker."

Neil turned to Miss Lina with a question about Mr. Jason.

She smiled, "Mr. Jason's cabin is just below this house—there is a connection between them." She put an arm about his shoulders and handed him a pair of dark gloves. "Another secret, please, Cornelius?"

Neil nodded. Into his mind floated a remembrance of the envelope Mr. Rogers had given him to exchange for the mushrooms. . . .

Dr. Finley buttoned his jacket and pulled on gloves as Mr. Jason said, "I can help some with owl calls. It's a still night and sound should carry." He amazed them with a series of weird calls, mournful hoots, and quavering whistles.

"If you hear three hoots that will mean danger."

Neil was grateful for the steady hum of the frogs,

blending the deep drum of the bullfrog with the shrill tone of the peeper—perhaps they would help mask the noise underfoot.

As his eyes adapted to the dark, Neil realized it wasn't really pitch dark. He wondered where all the light was coming from on such a starless night and he was grateful for it. It helped them to move quickly.

After a time a sudden noise brought them to a stop. Finally Neil was able to point out a raccoon, squatting on a rock. They went on; the raccoon crashed into the undergrowth.

At first the night had seemed very cool; now Neil noticed he was comfortably warm. Their scent had been caught by a deer. There came her alarmed sneeze, and to make sure her clan heard she repeated the odd signal. They didn't see her; she disappeared in silence.

"How is it possible," Neil wondered, "for a deer to run without a sound while I cannot help making noise?"

It was a long while before Dr. Finley stopped and reached for Neil, behind him. They listened and heard, below on the level stretch of land, a man on horseback, There was no need for words. Both knew Sam Gunn was searching. They ran now whenever openings appeared in the trees.

Dr. Finley began shifting toward the river. Neil was glad for the protection of the rising mist; it helped to blur their movements. He was watching for the landmark—the Indian trail tree. It was a large oak that years before, as a sapling, the Indians had tied down with rawhide at a ninety-degree angle. Dr. Finley saw it and signaled. They turned straight down then to the river. Within yards of it they dropped to their hands and knees.

"Wait here. I don't want to take you into the nettles if I don't have to."

Neil tried to follow Dr. Finley's path through the great patch of giant nettles, but he could detect no movement at all. He waited, alert to any strange noise above the doleful sound of the tree frogs.

"It must," he thought, "have been hard, cooped up there, waiting for help. Waiting how long in the dark? Who had hollowed out this underground room without disturbing the growth of the nettles? Had they worked in the night, dumping the earth in the river?" He did not know and was relieved that Sam Gunn was not aware of its location at all.

After a while Neil sensed that Dr. Finley and the slave were moving toward him through the nettles. He turned back and could barely see their outlines as they crawled through the mist on their hands and knees. Upon reaching the trail tree, they stood. Dr. Finley and Neil put the slave between them, his arms around their shoulders, bearing his great weight.

"His breathing," Neil thought, "sounds trembly, as if he's been crying."

Neil was glad to gain the protection of the heavy woods. They could not move with the speed they had earlier, but still managed, an hour later, to reach the higher ground. Then, faintly, they heard an owl hoot of three notes. Dr. Finley pushed the slave down, taking no chances.

Neil dropped next to a large stone and willed himself to become a part of it. The hoofbeats were coming nearer. The rider had moved up from the level land into the woods, passing by on higher ground. They hurried then, taking less care to be quiet. Neil was sure it was growing lighter.

Again they heard the rider on his return sweep on the level land below and redoubled their efforts, hoping he would not swing back toward them. The owl cries were clearer now—they heard the three-note signal and dropped where they stood.

This time Neil could find no stone and rolled over to a log in such haste that the rough bark scratched and left its imprint. His heartbeats kept time with the hoof-beats of the approaching horse. The rider had chosen their section of the woods again. This time he swept by very close.

"Dear God," Neil prayed, "let us get to the house before he comes again." The morning light was gray.

Neil and Dr. Finley let go of the slave, goading themselves to greater hurry. They could hear the horse-man returning. This time they needed no warning owl cry. He was not sweeping by on the lower level. He was not coming toward them. He was coming from behind. And worse, they could hear the barking of bloodhounds.

All of them broke into a last despairing run. The roof of the house was visible through the trees. Neil ran until he thought his lungs would burst. When they neared the house he saw Miss Sarah out by the drive. She had opened the door to the smokehouse and was pointing to it. They threw themselves at the small door and she swung it shut and locked it.

Inside the tiny brick building, they collapsed in a

tangle of legs, gasping for breath. Soon they became aware of a great commotion outside. The hounds were barking at a furious rate, ending in an odd, tapering whine.

Between great pants Neil whispered, "The skunks are tied to the door."

Puzzled, they heard squawking noises.

"Seems an odd time to be killing chickens, ma'am," the horseman said.

"We have sickness here," they heard Miss Sarah say, "and have need of broth. I will thank thee to remove thy noise from this place."

Dr. Finley looked down at the slave's leg. The trouser leg was soaked in blood. He whispered, "She's killed chickens to cover the blood!"

When it was quieter Dr. Finley asked, "What is your name?"

"Jim, sir."

"We're going to have to fix that leg, Jim, right away."

Not until the horseman had hurriedly crossed the bridge toward the village did Miss Sarah unlock the door. She pointed to a length of white muslin laid on the ground. They ran on it, across the drive. Then Miss Lina laid another piece of muslin and they ran across that to the side porch.

Mr. Jason came behind, rolling up the cloth as fast as he could. He took it to the cellar where he plunged it into tubs of cold water to rinse away the blood.

Miss Sarah helped Jim to a couch in a room off the kitchen and Dr. Finley began washing his hands. Miss Lina brought her scissors and cut away Jim's bloody trouser leg. To Neil, Jim seemed even larger than he had appeared in the woods.

"Cornelius, will thee carry this basin of water, please?" Miss Sarah brought soap and soft towels and began washing Jim's leg.

Neil asked Mr. Jason, coming up from the cellar, "Why did we have to walk on the cloth, sir?"

"So the bloodhounds can't track you to the house."

"They've gone."

"They'll be back."

We Pluck This Flower, Safety

Neil listened to Dr. Finley. "This leg has to be cleaned out and stitched or you'll bleed to death. I'll do it as fast as I can."

"Yes, sir."

"Hold his hands, Neil. This is the boy you have to thank for being here at all, Jim."

Mr. Jason held one leg, Miss Sarah the other. Neil could see the beat of Jim's heart at the base of his throat. When Dr. Finley began stitching, Jim clenched his teeth, the veins in his neck standing out like cords. Neil's hands were caught in a bone-crushing grip.

When it was over, Miss Sarah put a pillow beneath Jim's leg. Miss Lina brought tea and fed him custard. Exhausted, Jim fell back on his pillow.

Their thoughts were so centered on Miss Van Vliet and on Jim's well-being that none of them could think of food beyond sipping hot tea.

Miss Sarah glanced up and said, "Thy single horseman has multiplied."

Two men on horseback, with hounds, were approaching slowly, watching for Ebenezer and Emmaline. Neil hoped this was the morning Emmaline would allow her five babies to hop out and survey the world.

Dr. Finley stood up, reaching for his hat. "Sam Gunn is not taking another man from Niles."

Miss Lina quickly brought his bag. Miss Sarah helped Jim from the couch.

"Mr. Jason, get Jim down cellar. They may force their way in." Dr. Finley picked up a hammer and tacks and went out the front door. "What do you men think you're doing here?"

"There's a slave hidden here and we intend to search the house," one of the men said.

Serenely, Miss Lina faced them. "Thee is welcome to search if the doctor will allow it."

As if in answer, Dr. Finley took a sign from his bag and tacked it to the door. Its red letters said:

Quarantine
Diphtheria

He handed the hammer to Miss Lina, tipped his hat, and went on to the barn.

Looking first at the sign and then at one another, the men shook their heads and left, calling the hounds. Only then did Miss Sarah go to the barn to saddle her horse for Dr. Finley.

Neil asked, "How can you be so calm, Miss Lina?"

Miss Lina smiled. "We do not believe in slavery, Cornelius. Of course there are no slaves here. Now we'll see what Sam Gunn does when his men report the quarantine notice."

Mr. Jason helped Jim back to his couch and Neil went to the porch to watch Emmaline's babies. He also watched the road, hoping for news. Miss Sarah brought a plate of cookies and they nibbled away for thirty minutes before they saw Dr. Finley, coming at a fair pace toward the house.

"Did they find Miss Van Vliet?" Neil called.

Dr. Finley nodded and came bounding up the steps. "She's fine," and he put his arm about Neil's suddenly shaking shoulders. "You were right! She was in the cellar and you heard a mewing sound because she was gagged. They tied her to a post. She was thirsty, and angry, and frightened of the rats, but she's all right."

"Did Mr. Lord get help?" Miss Sarah asked.

"Clay and his father helped. Clay watched the back door all day from the riverbank and they were just going in when they saw Mr. Lord."

"Good old Clay! Lucky they got her out before Sam Gunn came back."

"Miss Van Vliet and Clay are waiting at my house, and I promised to bring you as soon as I could, Neil."

Miss Lina, watching at the door, said, "Thee has brought thy friends again."

Dr. Finley peered over her shoulder. "That's Sam Gunn. Three men with him—he means business!"

Miss Lina asked, "Shall we get Jim down cellar?"

"Not yet. Get your bonnets, quickly. You're going to Brother Levi's."

"How?"

"On the *Davy Crockett,* along with Neil's aunt and uncle. You will accompany a casket to a funeral, and Jim will be in the casket."

Jim appeared in the doorway, his eyes round.

"You'll be more comfortable than you were last night, Jim." Dr. Finley felt Jim's forehead.

Sam Gunn and his men seemed much surprised then to see Mr. Lord, Bible in hand, come riding behind them. Behind him, dressed in black, Esau Shepherd and Mr. Alexander drove the splendid hearse with four black horses wearing plumes.

Dr. Finley took Jim's arm. "Look through this curtain. Esau Shepherd made that hearse and he was up all night making a casket for you with a sliding panel so that you can look out. We needed an extra-large one."

Neil saw Uncle Bert's buggy driving into the yard and watched as his uncle helped Aunt Annie down. She was wearing her black dress, carrying a bouquet of tulips amidst stalks of fern, and crying! Uncle Bert kept patting her shoulder—Neil could scarcely believe his eyes.

Aunt Annie came in and hugged Neil. "Uncle Bert and I are so proud. Mr. Lord told us all about it."

Mr. Lord said, "I watched Sam Gunn when you drove in. He's really puzzled; he's never seen you two before. You're making it entirely believable."

Miss Sarah sent them a welcoming smile and gave Neil a large handkerchief. "Use this, Cornelius, to cover thy face."

The men carried the casket in and Miss Sarah quickly placed a blanket and pillow in the bottom while Miss Lina brought biscuits and a bottle of water.

Jim's eyes, intent, looked from one face to another.

144

He whispered, "Thank you." When he looked at Neil he reached deep into his pocket and took out a small coin. He offered it to him.

"It is likely all he has in the world," Neil thought, his chest in turmoil, but he accepted it without hesitation. "Thank you. If you send word, I'll write."

Jim nodded and climbed into the casket. Uncle Bert looked at Neil solemnly and winked; Neil knew he had done right to take the coin.

Esau Shepherd showed Jim how to slide the panel and Mr. Lord said, "I'll see that nothing is between you and the rail, Jim."

Dr. Finley placed a pillow beneath Jim's leg and closed the lid. "Move as quickly as you can. They may rush us."

Mr. Alexander said, "We've five men to their four. I'd like to see 'em try!"

Neil thought, "Six to their four, counting me."

Mr. Lord went out first and opened the door of the hearse. Uncle Bert, Dr. Finley, Esau Shepherd, and Mr. Alexander all groaned as they tried lifting the heavy casket. When they had it steadied, Neil opened the front door for them. He was thankful that Mr. Jason had moved Ebenezer to the side porch to join his family; at least that entrance was well protected. Ebenezer, with all the goings and comings of the morning at the front door, would have been worn out with stamping his feet and waving his tail.

Neil escorted Miss Lina and Miss Sarah to their buggy. He heard the men talking about him as he stepped up into the buggy and prepared, proudly, to drive.

"Where did that kid come from? I didn't see him go in."

Uncle Bert helped Aunt Annie, who was weeping fresh, zestful tears. Watching her, Neil used his handkerchief to cover his face.

Mr. Lord led the procession on horseback. Esau and Mr. Alexander followed with the hearse. Neil swung into line, with Uncle Bert's buggy coming after. Dr. Finley, also on horseback, brought up the rear. Close behind, Sam Gunn and his men followed. Neil was tense, wishing he had eyes in the back of his head. He could hear the bell of the arriving *Davy Crockett* pealing out, down river.

Mr. Jason was at the bridge, with his basket of catnip, for all the world an interested bystander. Neil guessed he had been there for some time in order to warn any driver not to cross and hold up the funeral procession.

People were standing at attention as the hearse passed, and men were removing their hats. They talked in small clusters, wondering who had died. Someone at the Quakers'? Diphtheria, did you say? Or scarlet fever? Oh, dear God!

The group waited as Dr. Finley went up the plank to talk to the captain of the *Davy Crockett.* Quickly the two men came back down and the captain directed getting the heavy casket aboard, passing the crowd of passengers waiting respectfully in the presence of death. Sam Gunn and his men tried to board, but the captain told them bluntly to stand aside while the funeral party was served. After the ladies had been escorted over the plank, the captain roped off that portion of the deck, placing two crewmen on guard. He made Sam Gunn stand at the far end.

"Sam Gunn's not looking happy 'bout that rope," Esau murmured.

Dr. Finley winked. "The captain is our friend, Esau. He said he will allow no one off the boat at Berrien except one messenger with a note for Brother Levi. And Brother Levi will be ready to board the boat when it docks at Shaker Farm."

Esau looked puzzled.

Mr. Alexander explained, "Only the funeral party will be allowed to leave the boat at Shaker Farm, Esau. Sam Gunn's not leaving. The same men who were in the posse that chased Sam Gunn are going to board and I'd like to see Sam's face as he watches them come up the plank."

"I'm not sure," Dr. Finley added, "how gentle they'll be when Brother Levi tells them how Sam Gunn treated Miss Van Vliet and Mr. Rogers. Some of those men aren't Shakers!"

"Sam Gunn," Neil thought, "hasn't a chance against both Aunt Annie and Brother Levi."

They stood, watching the boat move slowly down river and around the bend. Neil's eyes were on Uncle Bert and Aunt Annie, guarding the casket. He would have liked to whoop aloud in pride. He wished he could have gone; it would have been fun to surprise his friend, Francis Marion Ives.

Dr. Finley tied the horses behind Uncle Bert's buggy and climbed in. In the quietness of the moment, broken only by the steady clip-clop of the horse's hooves, Neil felt as though he were seeing with new eyes, as if he'd

147

been away a long time; the world seemed extraordinarily green. He felt inside his pocket to be sure of the coin.

"I will always keep this," he thought. "Always. I'll keep it in the box with my Indian arrowheads."

Suddenly, as if his heart had been pierced, he knew these months were ended, the coin his only tangible memory of great love and courage.

Dr. Finley said, when they stopped at the house, "Tell Mrs. Finley that I've gone over to check on Mr. Rogers and let him know all that's happened. Any message you want to send, Neil?"

Neil climbed down and untied the horses. "Tell him I'm coming to see him as soon as you'll let me. Oh— you might tell him I'm going to the bookstore for a copy of *Romeo and Juliet.*"

Dr. Finley looked surprised.

Neil grinned. "He'll be pleased, sir."